Love's *TWISTED* Diary

Kris Dean asserts the moral right to be identified as the author of this work.

© 2019 Love's Twisted Diary by Kris Dean

I would like to thank all of my friends and family that have not only supported me but encouraged me to follow my dream of becoming a writer. Without your support and love I wouldn't be where I am today, so, thank you!

I have always dreamed about becoming a writer since the age of 10. Over the years I have written many short stories and screenplays which I have never followed up on, until now.

Follow me:
Author website: www.krisdean.co.uk
Book website: www.lovestwisteddiary.co.uk
Facebook: www.facebook.com/krisdeanwriter

HAVE YOU EVER FELT LIKE
A DARK STORM IS COMING?

Love's *TWISTED* Diary

BY Kris Dean

INTRODUCTION

I'm going to tell you a story, a story that shook the god-dam earth that I stand on, a story that still severely psychologically batters my friends and I nearly twenty years later.

Firstly, I'm Mike, Mike Miller a 34-year-old SINGLE (yes I put that in caps) SINGLE guy. I work as a scriptwriter for my local radio station and live in a quaint village in the borough of Boston, Lincolnshire. I'm 5ft 10...

Hey, wait a sec this is seriously starting to sound like I'm writing some sort-of profile for tinder! Right enough of that drivel. Back to what I was on about before.

To get the whole story I am going to have to take you back, all the way back to the winter of 1999 or how we spelled it back then '9T9!' In fact, more specifically Saturday 6th November 1999, sorry, O.C.D kicking in there!

Back then, I had a somewhat unusual group of friends. There was Jay, A pretty level-headed guy, calculated, tall, and for some odd reason, one which I could never understand, always seemed to be popular with the WOMEN! Well, sixth form and college hotties.

Rick, a confident, sporty lad, he was pretty good at kicking everyone's ass at Football, oh, and certainly knew how to work his way around an engine. (a car engine before anyone gets any other ideas!)

Graham! Well, where do I begin with that vile cretin. In the words of the urban dictionary; A Person that is: brainless, stupid, child-like, and full of pointless information that makes no sense and appeals only to other cretins. Oh, and was absolutely full of SHIT! I, we, nicknamed him as Jasmine. He was a self-proclaimed sex god! (yes we all know one) And claimed to have had sex with more than half of the world's female population of humans and frequently made a right tit of himself. More about 'IT' later!

Finally. There was me! A fun-loving, shy, yet confident curtain-haired 90's boy band wannabe. Oh my god, the hair! Looking back on it from past photographs I looked so stupid, to make matters worse, it was bleached blonde!

So,

Saturday 6th November '9T9'

We (Rick, Jay, Jasmine and one's self) were hanging out at the annual bonfire and fireworks night, a yearly event which was organized by a group of bible bashers from our nearest town! Boring for some. However, if you think back to those days there was no such thing as the internet, well, there was, but it was the crappy dial-up which seemed to take a millennia to connect. And finally after waiting for ages to go online, it would be extremely slow, or I would have my mother whining at me because she wanted to use the phone.

Social media didn't exist, and mobile phones were only just starting to come in, which was great, but seriously try getting a bloody signal with those bricks! So, as you can imagine we were all limited for entertainment.

We just wandered the streets for hours, played football, destroyed plenty of hedges, pissed of Paedo Paul (more about him later) and chilled out playing various games on our latest consoles. Oh, and for Halloween that year Graham had a right stupid idea and robbed the local bakery of over three hundred eggs. He decided to 'go egging cars' one of which happened to hit a police car! So, as you could imagine we had almost the entire force after us, the dog's the lot! How the hell we managed not to get caught that night was nothing more than a miracle!

So anyway, nights like this were pretty good for entertainment, along with the weekly youth club and monthly discos.

As you could imagine nights like this didn't attract just us, it attracted some pretty fit tottie, and as 16-year-old sixth formers, we were most certainly in our element. That year it was full of the sixth form and college girls, and as usual Graham was making a total prick of himself,

"Oh, she'd get it, oh shagged her, oh fingered her, Rammed that, dirty slag, gave her a right mott job." Were the words coming out of his vile mouth!

He wasn't whispering either. He was talking loudly, very loudly and pointing at different girls while saying that!
Seriously, this dude is a court case waiting to happen! Quite frequently though we managed to catch him out with his bullshit and did we give him hell?
Yes, we did - Public humiliation came to mind!

So, as he was STILL going on about how he would 'ram his battle rod' into one's front bottom, someone caught my eye in the distance, someone who made my heart melt within an instant, that one person who would give my stomach the butterflies every time I saw her or heard her name mentioned. Gemma Wells! Oh she was the girl of my dreams. I had fancied her for years and years, but being the shy person I was I had never previously had the bottle to ask her out! Every time I spoke to her I would come over all nervous and end up stuttering – what a great way to win over a woman's heart!

But anyway, unfortunately for me she had a boyfriend – or so I thought! Something which Graham was about to correct me on!
But first, let me tell a bit about this baboon of a boyfriend. His name is Franko Cunningham, a 6ft four rugby player and bare-knuckle boxer, built like a tank and is an absolute psychopath! How Gemma saw anything in that prick was seriously beyond me! Anyway, back to the story.

As we were walking toward the abnormally tall bonfire the organizers had lit, seriously, looking back at it there should have been some sort of safety regulation breach, it was tall and narrow, the damn thing was leaning over!

Gemma and her friend Zoe began to walk toward us. I remember thinking, oh my god she's so gorgeous! That beautiful long blonde hair, those amazing hazel eyes you could just get lost in! Oh, and what an ass! No seriously what an ass, she was just perfect!
As she walked past us, as usual, I could not help but glare at her in amazement, she also glanced at me, flicked her hair with her hand and smiled at me, I smiled back.

and then...

BANG!

I was on my ass! As 110% of my attention was on her, I only went and walked into a bloody telegraph pole! How embarrassing! And guess what? Not only was everyone bloody laughing at me, Gemma saw everything! What a tool I thought! Although, the expression on Gemma's face told me that she did seem somewhat concerned about me, but with me being the man, I got up, brushed myself down and pretended that my jaw didn't feel like it had been detached!

   "You're such a bellend, Mike!"
Jay said while wiping the tears of laughter away from his face!

   "Oh shut up" I replied.

We just carried on walking toward the bonfire, making sure we didn't get too close as it looked as if it could topple over at any given moment, so we just waited at a safe distance in anticipation of the grand firework display!

"Why don't you just ask her out mate?" asked Rick,

"What do you mean?" I replied,

"Gemma, it's so obvious you like her" Rick stated,

"Nah" I sighed - "She would never go for someone like me, besides she's going out with that buffoon"

"No, she ain't" interrupted Graham,

"What do you mean she isn't?" I asked, totally puzzled!

"That she isn't!" came his sarcastic reply,

"Since when?" I asked,

"About three weeks I think!" Graham replied,

"Three bloody weeks! Three bloody weeks! And you never thought of mentioning anything to me?"

I couldn't help but voice the anger in my response,

"I forgot!" Replied Graham in his dumb kinda tone!

"You forgot! So the girl I have lusted over for the past three years splits up with her boyfriend and you 'forgot' to mention it to me!" I couldn't help but shout!

I was in shock, I couldn't believe what I was hearing! OMG, What a brainless ghoul! Seriously, Graham took the word 'stupid' to a whole new level!

That anger didn't last long before the feeling of relief came over me, a window of opportunity had arisen! Gemma was single! Now is my chance, I remember thinking. All of a sudden I had all the confidence in the world, nothing was going to stop me, I must find her, I must tell her how I feel about her (in a non-pervy kind of way) I thought, and off I went – believing that my life was about to change!

I spent a good half an hour looking around for Gemma, I checked the barn, walked back around to the bonfire, (kept my distance) checked the car park, she was nowhere. I was slightly saddened by the fact that I couldn't find her, but there was plenty of time to tell her. The following Friday would be youth club night, so at least I had six days to compose myself and figure out exactly what I was going to say to her.

Out of the blue, shockingly I was pulled back and forcefully spun around.

Facing me was Franko!

He stood staring at me with his piercing dark eyes, he stepped forward and got right into my face, I couldn't help but notice his deep scar which cut through his left cheek, I could sense his pure rage and mental sickness, I knew he meant business. Fear, complete fear took over me, I froze to the spot where I stood! Adrenaline was pumping through my veins, my heart was pounding!

"I have seen the way you look at my woman!" Franko spat through his clenched teeth.

I tried to respond but couldn't get my words out – he put his hand around my neck and squeezed, partially cutting off my airway.

"You better stay away from her, if I catch you anywhere near her you will get this" Spat Franko.

He looked down, unzipped his jacket and released me. I peered down inside his coat, I was shocked, he had a handgun in his inner pocket!

"Understand me?" said Franko.

He backed off, closed his jacket, turned and walked away leaving me frozen, trembling and sick with fear.

Monday 8th November '٩T٩'

For the remainder of that weekend, I felt like someone had rammed their fist through my chest, twisted and pulled my heart out!
I had hardly slept, whenever I did drift off I abruptly woke with night terrors and soaked with sweat! I was a wreck, never in my life until that point had I ever received a threat like that, the frightening thing was that he would actually do it!
Monday morning came around far too quickly, and unfortunately, it was time for school! I tried, pleaded, and begged for mother not to make me go to school, but she had none of it! Unless I was dying of Ebola or some other mutation I had to go!

As I dragged my feet along the corridor on the way to my first lesson of the day Rick, Graham and Jay couldn't help but notice my puffy panda eyes, and the fact that I looked as pale as a bed sheet.

   "Dude are you okay?" asked Jay,

I was too cut up and tired even to reply,

   "You haven't got diarrhea, have you?" asked Graham,

   "Piss off" I replied.

Although my stomach did feel dodgy, however, that was because of stress and lack of beauty sleep.

Jay, much to my anguish, asked me what Franko had spoken to me about on Saturday. Oh my god, I thought he hadn't noticed, I was just hoping it would have gone unnoticed. The plan was simple, keep quiet, stay away from Gemma, never speak to her again and only pray that I never saw him again! Failing that I would have swiftly moved in with my dad who lived over 200 miles away! No way could he have found me there! But no, Jay just had to throw a bloody grenade into the mix! Well, that just set my anxiety off! I felt sick and even worse – I needed the toilet, badly!

Struggling to hold my nerves, without saying another word I legged it back down the corridor to find the nearest toilet, but as usual, nothing in my life could be that simple!
As I was running around the corner, I only went and ran into Gemma, poleaxing her straight to the floor!

   "Oh my god! Gemma I'm so sorry!" I said, feeling concerned that I may have hurt her.

I helped her up from the floor and being the kind-hearted woman she was, she saw the funny side to it,

   "Where are you going to in such a hurry?" She asked.

Obviously, I wasn't going to tell her that the whole world was about to fall out of my arsehole, so, I just came up with the lame excuse that I was late for class!

As I gazed into her eyes, my nerves started to settle, I was calming down, it felt so right being in her presence, what the hell was this feeling I felt? It was something I certainly had never felt before.

I could literally feel the electricity running through my body. Gemma then asked if I was going to the youth club on Friday, oh my god it brought it all back with a vengeance. What if he was going to be there? What if he found out I was speaking with her? I began to sweat!

"Of course," I said nervously,

"Ah that's fantastic, I look forward to seeing you there then" Gemma replied confidently.

I couldn't take it any longer. I had to go, I literally had to go! So, without even saying goodbye or giving any explanation, I just ran, leaving Gemma looking stunned and very confused!

After spending an hour in the sick room with nurse Debbie, who was trying to calm me down and failing, she had no other choice but to call my mother and ask her to come and pick me up and take me home!

Once I got home, I spent the rest of the day escaping the world and its pressures. Laid in my back garden gazing up at the sky watching the transition from daylight to twilight, how the clouds began to darken and the wind picking up. Listening to its howl as it blew through the trees which caused them to creak was somewhat therapeutic.

Lying there on the cold earth, I didn't realize how chilly I had become. As I took a deep breath in, I tried to gather my thoughts and reconnect myself. I sat up, stretched and looked up at what was around me. Not only could I see an impending storm in the distance, I could smell the rain to come.

Something then caught my attention, a noise, a footstep. I felt my heart rate quicken, a fight or flight response kicked in. I spun my head around to face a potential threat! To my relief, it was Jay!

"You alright mate, you seem edgy? Not like you to be laid here?" said Jay.

I couldn't muster the words to tell him, and I felt like if I did something terrible might happen, would he be angry? Disappointed?
It's not like I couldn't trust him as he was my best friend, we had been friends since we were five years old!

Jay walked over and sat down next to me without saying another word. We sat there for a few minutes in silence listening to the sound of the wind and the claps of thunder from the distant storm. Jay rudely interrupted my concentration,

"Storms coming mate!"

I looked up, and turned my head toward him,

"Obviously!" I replied,

"Come on, what's up mate?" Jay asked.

I took a deep breath in and to my surprise, the words just fell out of my mouth, I told him everything! Some of it probably didn't even make sense as I was too overcome with anxiety for it to even make sense.

Finally, the words stopped, I stopped. I felt relieved in knowing that someone else knew, but I couldn't look at him! I was too overcome with emotion, and what would he think?

Would he laugh it off? Take it seriously? Tell me to forget about Gemma?

Jay just sat there in shock for a few moments which felt like an eternity.

   "Wow mate, that's why you haven't been yourself today and just laying there like a soft spud in this weather!"

Jay's humour soon dried up. His voice was overcome with concern and anger.

   "Why didn't you tell me sooner? Have you told anyone else? Your parents? Gemma?"

At that point with Jay's questions, it became too much, the tears fell from my face! I tried to resist them to not seem soft. Jay wanted to reassure me,

   "Mate, its all just empty threats. He won't do anything, and I've got your back!"

However, I wasn't taking any of it. Jay knew what Franko was like as most people in our age group feared him and now I was fixed on his radar, not only that but I had deep feelings for Gemma but couldn't do anything about them.
Jay was firm, trying to reassure me that I should ignore Franko's threats and to simply go for it!

A small part of me knew he was right. That if I liked her as much as I did, then I should at least find out if she fancied me in any way. So, me being the shy person I was, I asked Jay if he could have a little word with her, just to drop her a tiny teenie hint that I fancied her to see what reaction he got!

Surprisingly, Jay reluctantly agreed! Usually, Jay didn't like to play cupid, but in this particular circumstance, he said that he would only do it that one time, but never again! I started to feel a little more optimistic, a bit more positive about the future.

At a click of a finger, the heavens opened, and monsoon-like rain fell from the sky! Both of us quickly stood up, legged it inside the house and played on my football game for the rest of the evening. Having Jay there with me certainly helped calm me down, I had somebody to talk to, it felt so much better knowing that someone else knew.

Thursday 25th November '9T9'

A couple of weeks had passed with no incident or a brutal beating from Franko, and things were thankfully quiet on that subject.

Everything was finally just about back to normal. I had the confidence to go out again without having to take diazepam, which I stole from mother's prescription to calm me down, seriously that stuff was brutal! I had never slept so well in my life, so yeah, I was pretty happy!

That being said! There was a couple of things winding me up, one, Graham! Listening to that fool continually talking about vaginas and quite worryingly, women's bum-holes! I can't remember the exact details as I just tried to switch off from all the bull that came out of his vile mouth, however, it did sound like he had a deranged sexual encounter with a woman that resembled a hairy silverback! Christ that lad had severe issues!

Secondly, Jay had been continuously going on, and on about me asking Gemma out! Well, here we go, drum roll, please...

A few days after my 'mental breakdown' Jay managed to get Gemma on her own, casually mentioned that I fancied her, and guess what! She liked me too! Oh my days! I was over the moon, what a fantastic feeling, it was like my entire bucket list had been ticked off. BUT, there was just one snag! I didn't have the bottle (as of yet) to ask her out!

I had been going over and over it in that brain of mine. Do I ask her out? Do I ask her out on a date? Or meet up a few times so we could get to know each other?

I certainly was not taking Graham's advice of, well, I'm not going to go there! Anyway, the pressure from Jay was becoming quite unbearable and somewhat embarrassing!

We had entered the last ten minutes of the lunch break at school. Jay, Graham and myself were gathered around the back of the geography block, a building that stood away from the courtyard and main school building. I was nervous, so nervous, bloody Graham was caning back a cigarette.

"Why do it, Jasmine? One, your gonna ruin your health and two, what if we get bloody caught?" I said,

"Oh shut up and stop being so hormonal" Was Graham's response.

Hormonal? Seriously? I honestly don't think I was the one with hormone issues there! I was, however, about to get some satisfactory payback from that comment as Gemma and Zoe were walking toward us.
I remember thinking, please don't talk to me, please don't talk to me, not in front of this lot anyway.

Jay and I had seen the two girls walking toward us, however, Graham had not! Still dragging on his cancer stick and blabbering on about his Silverback encounter, Gemma began to creep up behind Graham, once she got close enough she shouted,

"Graham Gullard, put that cigarette out immediately!"

Well, Graham let out an almighty shriek and threw his cigarette over the fence! I had never heard a bloke let out such a girly screech in my entire life!
That was it, I was howling! Creased up with laughter! It was the funniest thing I had seen in a long time! Jay and the girls were laughing too, Graham, left all red-faced didn't know where to put himself and for the first time in his life, left speechless!

Even until this day, he hasn't lived that one down!

The school bell then rang out, signaling the end of the break. Well, I call it a school bell, it sounded more like a droning sound from a battleship!

OMG, the damn thing was deafening. Seriously, it felt like my eardrums were about to pop when it went off close to me. So at that, we all made our way back to the main building to attend class, still laughing and joking at Graham's girly screech.

Friday 26th November '9T9'

Friday evening had finally arrived, the night we had all been looking forward to all week, the youth club! A night for us all to chill out, laugh, play some football, and be away from aggy parents, and for me, it was D-Day! The day I had planned to ask Gemma out for a date! I was nervous, but excited. Quite considerably I had been feeling the pressure building, and would be finally relieved to get it off my chest. But just to make the need to ask her a tad more urgent, the Christmas Disco date had been announced for Saturday 11th December! Everyone, I mean everyone would be scrambling around trying to find a date, so, I had to get in there quick!

The Christmas disco was the most significant event of the year. More importantly for us, that particular year would be the last chance to go as once we had turned 17, we wouldn't have been able to attend as this specific youth club, and discos were for 15 to 17-year-olds only. Shame, but at least then we were to be in the world of nightclubs, pubs, and house/college parties. Oh, and of course, being able to get served alcohol!

As we (Jay, Rick, Graham and I) strutted around the youth club confidently looking for other people to play a game of footie with us I couldn't help but notice a stunning young woman walk through the entrance of the youth club, it was Gemma, and oh my god she looked terrific! She wore a stunning tight blue dress, had her hair in a loose perm, oh my, she really had made an effort! (not saying she never made an effort because she did) however that particular night she looked even more amazing!

Instinctively, Jay noticed that I was just stood staring at her, with an almost possessed like look on my face.

"Go talk to her then dude," Jay said.

Without saying a word back, I slowly made my way over to where Gemma stood. While weaving through the crowds of people I began to get butterflies in my stomach, I could feel my heart pumping faster and faster as I got closer to her, but this was it, there was no turning back now.

"Hey Gemma, how are you?" I said nervously,

"Oh, hey Mike, I'm great, how are you?" replied Gemma,

"Yeah I'm good thanks, I must say you look amazing tonight!" I said,

"Ah thanks Mike, you look good yourself!" Gemma replied.

Wow, well that got that out of the way, and she thought I looked good as well, amazing! The nerves died away in an instant, a sudden wave of confidence overcame me, if I could accomplish this then I could take on the world, no problem!

"Aw thank you, I don't suppose I could have a chat with you could I?" I asked,

"Yeah sure, no problem" Gemma replied,

We both made our way outside. Suddenly, I became all edgy again, I needed to keep it together, I had planned for this moment for years! It was like the biggest single opportunity I ever had. I remember thinking, Don't mess it up, don't mess it up! And had to be quick about it as it was bloody freezing, and poor Gemma was only wearing a dress.

Stood to the left of us was a girl called Grace from my class at school. Ideally, I didn't want anyone to earwig in on what I wanted to say, just in case I got rejected or something, but surprisingly, I didn't care, it was like it was meant to be.

"Sorry to drag you out here Gem, but I needed to ask you something," I said,

"That's okay, what would you like to ask me?" she replied while shivering from the crisp wind,

"I was wondering if you had a date for the disco yet?" I asked nervously,

"No, not yet Mike" replied Gemma,

"Ah okay, I was wondering, erm if you, erm."

Oh my god, I was bottling it, the palms of my hands began to sweat! I had a sudden hot flush, became dizzy and I could feel my tongue becoming all dry. Hold it together, hold it together, hold it fucking together, you can do this! Were my thoughts, compose, chill, BREATHE!

"I was wondering if you would be my date for the disco?" I asked hastily.

There we go, you did it! I thought, thank god that was over, but what was she going to say? The suspense was killing me. Gemma turned her head and looked to the floor. Her response seemed negative! I felt defeated, I panicked!

"Its okay, Gem, sorry, its okay, erm, sorry I bothered you, lets just..."

Gemma interrupted,

   "Of course I will, I thought you'd never ask!" she replied.

What did she say? Had I heard that correctly? Oh my god, she said yes! Really? Am I dreaming?
I pinched myself, no! I was still awake! My god, likc the best looking girl I had ever met, just said yes to my proposal! I felt like the king of the world, nothing else mattered, I needed to make this work!

   "Ah brilliant!" I said with a tremendous amount of relief.

Then came that awkward moment, do I give her a quick peck?

No! No! That's something Graham would do, the creep. So instead, I gave her a quick hug, and she was freezing bless her,

   "Right, let's get back inside you're freezing!" I said to her.

As we walked back inside Grace gave me such a dirty look, what the hell was she staring at the stupid bitch? But I didn't care. I was the architect of my kingdom at that moment in time, nothing was going to bother me!

We made our way back inside, mutually we wanted to go back to our friends, she went back to Zoe, and I went back to the guys smiling away like a Cheshire cat, Jay looked over and saw me grinning to myself,

"Ah mate, I take it all went well?" said Jay,

"Oh yes!" I replied confidently,

"Fantastic news pal," said Rick.

Graham, had to spoil the occasion.

"Ah Mike's gonna get his willy wet, get in there boy!" He shouted out.

He just had to ruin it didn't he, the prick! Seriously, why the hell did we hang around with him? It must be because we felt sorry for him or something.

"Reminds me of the time I shagged Holly Clare!" Graham continued,

Holly Clare, seriously? Now that was a new low! Holly Clare was famously known as the school bike, she was like that top piece of bread that everyone touched, but nobody wanted.

"You shagged Holly Clare?" Said Rick,

"Yup" replied Graham,

"What a load of bull!" I said,

"You're just jealous!" said Graham

"What, jealous that your gonna catch some sort of mutated killer crab and I'm not? Yeah right!" I replied.

Conveniently, Holly Clare and her chavvy mates just happened to walk by us. Graham, without realizing Holly was there, stated,

"You're just all jealous that I shagged Holly Clare and you fuckers didn't!"

As Graham went on to explain to us how he had 'pulverized' her already half-beaten vagina, Holly could hear everything, the look on her face was just pure disgust!

"This is going to be interesting" I whispered to Jay.

Well, Holly had heard enough of Graham's in-depth description. She just let rip at him, calling him all the names under the sun, saying that he's full of crap and that she'd never sleep with him amongst other things I'm not going to repeat!

She then slapped him across the face, so hard that I could almost feel the impact myself. Holly walked away leaving Graham red-faced and embarrassed, with a lovely hand mark across his right cheek!

I was laughing so hard I could have cried! What an idiot! There should be a new type of mental condition given to him, bullshitteritious sprang to mind!

That was it, Graham up and left. Jay and Rick felt sorry for him, but I certainly didn't! As I said to them, he was so full of shit! Yeah, he's an alright lad when he's on his own, but just liked to show off excessively in front of people, he didn't do himself any good whatsoever!

Come on, he claimed that once he saw a bumble bee that was nearly a foot long, Really? Anyway, enough of that let's concentrate on the good news; I had a date with Gemma! Finally!

For the rest of that night Jay, Rick and I played a couple of games of footie, chatted and laughed away with Gemma and Zoe. All in all, a fantastic day and evening!

Monday 29th November '9T9'

Monday morning soon rolled around, and it was time to get ready for school! I was buzzing, never before had I ever looked forward to a school day like I did that morning!
I had spent the weekend playing football with the lads, taping the UK top 40 from the radio, oh, and texting Gemma, so much that I used up a whole ten pound top up card!

I couldn't believe how much we had in common. We liked the same type of music, both of us was into writing, the same kind of films and both wanted very similar outcomes in life, such as college, uni, etc. The only thing she couldn't quite understand was my feelings of excitement that still engulfed me regarding that famous treble win by my favourite football team back in May that year. Oh, and my weird obsession with yo-yo's, YES, yo-yo's! Come on! They were in trend back then!

   Once at school, the first lesson was P.E. I hated P.E with a passion!
It wasn't because of the sports we played because I enjoyed those, no, it was because the teacher was a grumpy arsehole!
To make matters worse, I had to put up with Graham! And he just merely clung onto me like a needy toddler!

As usual, the teacher was late, leaving us all trembling to the bone in the cold! It was freezing, easily the coldest morning of the winter so far!
Through the chattering of my teeth I could smell something rancid,

   "Jasmine, have you farted?" I asked,

   "NO!" Graham replied abruptly.

I knew he was telling the truth as he usually would own up to producing something that smelt like raw sewage, so where the hell was that stench coming from? I thought, anyway the teacher had finally arrived, in his usual 'arsehole' mood. Before even letting us inside, he just had read out the register outside, leaving us all to freeze just that little bit more, I swear he used to do it on purpose!

Finally, inside the changing rooms after twenty minutes of waiting and possibly catching hypothermia in the process, we got changed into our P.E gear.

That day was basketball, so at least we were going to be inside in the warmth. Graham did his usual routine of waiting for everyone to clear off so he could hide his cigarettes inside his shoes, forcing me to stay with him in case he got caught, just so I could get in trouble too, yeah cheers for that mate!

As Graham put his packet of fags into his shoe, we finally figured out where that rancid smell was coming from. He had only gone and stepped in what looked like a year's worth of dog poo! Oh my god, it was gross!
Carefully, Graham picked up the shoe by its laces, looked at it carefully, then wretched!

   "Mate that's disgusting, get rid of it!" I said.

Still heaving with tears in his eyes, Graham frantically looked around for something to wipe it off with, walking around the changing room with the filthy shoe kept at arm's length, he struggled to find something to wipe it off with,

"Dude, get rid of it, it stinks!" I said,

   "Don't you think I fucking know that?" Graham said while still borking.

Graham couldn't find anything like tissue or wipes, so, he did something I didn't expect him to do! He wiped it all off with someone else's school trousers!

   "You can't do that Jasmine, stop it!" I said shockingly.

But it was too late, he had done it. As he finished a stern, deep voice shouted out which shocked us both to the bone, so much that I felt my heartbeat from within own wrists.

   "WHAT THE HELL DO YOU THINK YOU ARE DOING?!"

we both turned around. It was the teacher!

I thought to myself, OMG, Graham's going to be in so much trouble now! This is amazing!

The teacher fiercely snatched the soiled trousers away from Graham, grabbed him by the scruff of his shirt and marched him out of the building and headed toward the admin block. I couldn't help but giggle to myself as I knew how much trouble he was going to be in.

Word soon got around the school about the incident, it was certainly the topic of conversation for the rest of that day. I had so many requests for information from many different people for the rest of the day, it was hilarious, for the second time, Graham had now been caught out! Holly on Friday and now that! What was even better news, he had been suspended! Finally, we would have some peace!

Later on that evening I was at the park with Jay and Rick. Graham's parents had grounded him following his suspension from school, so he wasn't there – pure bliss! We were sat on the park bench talking about what had happened earlier that day. Dressed for the bone-chilling cold weather, we were all feeling as if we were ready to go home, after all, it was far too cold to be sitting around.
It was a dark, gloomy evening, the wind was light but the moon was full and high in the sky which illuminated everything around us, it was quite atmospheric. We got up from the bench and started to walk toward the car park which was the only exit from the park.

Suddenly! A car screeched into the car park, then became stationary with its full beam of light focussed on us, what the hell was this all about? I thought. We stopped in our tracks and looked into the blinding light for a few moments. Two more cars then came into the car park and pulled up alongside the first. I could faintly hear the engines of the vehicles ticking over. They did sound beefy, so I knew they were boy racer cars. It didn't feel right! In my gut, I knew something terrible was about to happen.

We stood in silence, facing the cars. The engines then shut off, followed by the lights which left me slightly dazzled with blind spots in my vision that seemed to form every time I blinked. I counted seven people in total that got out of the cars, with what looked like baseball bats and other shorter objects in their possession.

I couldn't see them very well because of the dim yellow street lamps which only slightly illuminated them. They began to walk toward us! We started to take steps backward. Then, they began to charge at us!

"RUN!" Jay screamed!

We all ran away in different directions! I headed toward the wooded area. As I ran at full speed, I had a quick glance behind me, I saw three members of the mysterious gang getting closer to me! Adrenaline kicked into my system, and I began to run faster, faster than I had ever run before, my heart was pounding through my chest and sweat was pouring down my face. Fear, terrible fear was taking over me like a virus attacking everything that it came into contact with!

I reached the tree line and just carried on running as fast as I could, hurdling over tree stumps and narrowly missing larger trees. As I got further into the woods, the inevitable happened, I tripped and twisted my ankle on a small fallen tree! The pain from the fall pulsated from my right ankle. I knew I had either twisted it badly or broke it. It began to burn, like a fleshy burn type of pain, but I couldn't cry out as I would have given away my whereabouts.
As the adrenaline pumped through my veins, I managed to drag myself along the floor and got myself positioned behind a large fallen tree.

As I tried to catch my breath, I heard faint footsteps! I could hear the crackle from fallen leaves and branches. They were getting louder! They were getting closer!

I could feel my heart thumping harder, I held my hand over my mouth to silence my heavy breathing. The footsteps were now just about on top of me, right in front of the stump I was cowered behind, then silence, complete silence, the footsteps had stopped. I closed my eyes and prayed that this wasn't the end, the end of my life, I'm gonna die, I'm gonna die, I remember thinking.

After a few moments of silence, I thought to myself, where had the footsteps gone? I couldn't hear anything apart from the breeze whistling through the trees and the slightest creak of their branches.

After another few minutes of silence, I slowly turned around, still in agony from my ankle I slowly peered over the top of the tree, scanning the area with an eagle eye. I couldn't see anyone, where the hell had they gone? Who the hell was it?
After a few more moments of silence, I built up the courage to try and stand. Carefully and cautiously I managed to pull myself up, and slowly hobble back the way I came from, staying alert to everything around me with my eagle eyes and hawk-like hearing.

As I approached the park, I heard the footsteps once more, fear suddenly set in, I quickly power-limped to the nearest tree, stood perfectly still with my back up against the stump and shut my eyes. The sound drew ever closer. I heard a faint whisper!

"Mike, Mike is that you?"

 To my relief, I knew that voice! It was Jay! I was elated! I opened my eyes, peeked my head around the tree and saw Jay and Rick stood there.

   "Boy am I glad to see you guys!" I said to them both,

   "Same here mate!" said Jay,

   "Who the fuck are they?" I asked,

   "I don't know, but they mean business" replied Jay,

We then heard the screeching of tires, we gazed through the remaining trees and saw the three cars wheel spin away. Sudden, much-needed relief overcame us, and for a while afterward we just sat there on the floor in silence. Thank god that was over with, but there were so many unanswered questions, who was it? What did they want? And why us?

What we didn't know and what I wish we knew back then, that this was just the beginning, that things were soon to become even darker and twisted.

Wednesday 8th December '9T9'

Two weeks had passed since the whole incident in the park, for that entire time, I had not left the house, not because I was scared, well partly! I was in plaster. I had chipped a bone in my ankle and had some ligament damage, so with doctors orders, I had a couple of weeks of perfect relaxation! Playing on the computer, listening to tunes and having my mates over in the evenings. Initially, it was bliss! However, just lately it had become boring, so fricking boring! I just wanted to get out and have a laugh with everyone, hearing stories like Graham getting slapped, yet again and I wasn't there to witness it, I was gutted as I used to enjoy seeing Graham getting caught out with his persistent lies!

On the positive side, it did give me some time to think, time to reflect on some of the things that had happened over the past few weeks. Gemma and I were getting on so well, better than I thought we would, it felt so right being around one and other and we were getting close, like very close!

With the disco being just a matter of days away I had planned on asking Gemma out in the right way, in the hope of us becoming an official couple. I had also thought about Franko. There was no doubt in my mind that it was that idiot and his mates that chased us through the woods but as Jay had said, he was only doing it because he liked to be in control. But no more, there was nothing that was going to stop my pursuit of love with Gemma and thought that with a bit of luck Franko would back off.

Unfortunately, I had to take a few more days 'bed rest' so, coincidentally my first outing would be the disco.

So, instead of me boring you about the day I was about to have I'm going to tell you about Gemma's day.

That morning Gemma and Zoe were waiting for the bus to pick them up for school. She told me that it was absolutely freezing, a bright but very bitter morning. While waiting for the bus to arrive, apparently I was one of the topics of conversation, she didn't tell me what she was talking to Zoe about me for which was surprising because she was usually so honest. All I knew was that it was disco related but no more. Secondly, she was talking to her about how her parent's arguments had intensified. Her parents were not in a good place. They had financial difficulties, her dad was drinking a lot, I say a lot, meaning it was most nights. It was such a shame because he was a lovely bloke, very welcoming. Things were getting that bad at home for her she was considering moving in with Zoe as it was severely affecting her studies. What also didn't help was that Franko was still texting her and trying to call, Gemma just ignored every text and phone call, but yet, it persisted, much to the annoyance of Gemma.

Grace, (Yes that same Grace that gave me evils, the divvy cow) interrupted the conversation that Gemma and Zoe were having. She sympathized with Gemma as her parents had gone through divorce years earlier, leaving her in a highly toxic family home with an alcoholic and drug addict older sister, a mother who didn't seem bothered about her daughters but much more interested in drinking and bringing different men home most weekends. That pulled on Gemma's heartstrings. She felt so sorry for her, it kind of summed things up for her that Grace's situation was far worse than her own. Gemma being Gemma then offered her friendship to Grace, they exchanged phone numbers and told Grace that if she ever needed anything she could give her a call.

Gemma went on to tell me about what had happened that evening, after a pretty uneventful day at school, she was on her way to meet Zoe. She was walking alone through a public footpath, surrounded only by trees and hedges. It was a blustery and cold evening, so much that her blonde hair was ferociously blowing around with the wind, forcing her to keep removing it from her face. She began to walk faster through the footpath which was a good half mile long. For one it was cold and just wanted to get to the warmth of Zoe's house, for two it was bloody creepy along there!

Gemma got halfway down the footpath when she heard a loud rustling noise come from the hedges, so loud that it made her stop and look. But there was nothing. She couldn't hear anything, must have been hearing things she thought. However, as she began to carry on walking a hooded figure stepped out in front of her then just stood to watch her!

She took a couple of steps backward! The hooded man took a couple of steps forward, and into the glow of the street lamp. It was Franko!

   "Oh Franko! You frightened me!" said a shaken up Gemma.

She was relieved it was Franko, as it could have easily been some mad serial killer or something. She didn't want to see Franko as she just wanted him out of her life, but at least it wasn't a serial killer!

   "What are you doing here? She asked,

   "Waiting for you!" said Franko,

Gemma was stunned at the response he gave, how on earth did he know where she was? And what the hell was he doing waiting in the bushes?

"Why are you following me around Franko?"

Franko lunged forward and grabbed Gemma's arm,

"Babe, we need to sort shit out, I want you back!" pleaded Franko,

Cautiously, Gemma removed Franko's large, scar ridden hands away from her arm,

"Franko, we're over, please accept that I'm sorry! I don't have those feelings anymore."

Franko huffed and puffed, he began to become frustrated,

"It's that dickhead Miller ain't it" He grunted,

"What about Mike?" Asked Gemma,

"I knew it, you two are fucking together, I knew the rumors were true!" shouted Franko,

Franko lost control and punched the lamp post, then kicked a tree! Breathing heavily with anger he awaited Gemma's response,

"Franko, I'm not seeing Mike, and even if I was, it has nothing to do with you because we are over!" shouted Gemma,

Franko simply ignored what Gemma had just said and carried on interrogating her,

"So, are you taking him to the disco?" asked Franko,

"Franko! Please stop it, what goes on between Mike and me has nothing to do with you, so please let me go and just let me get on with my life!"

Gemma brushed past Franko and carried on walking quickly along the footpath without looking back. She began to cry from the shock and frustration. All she wanted was to be able to move on with her life, to make something of us. With what was going on at home and now what Franko was doing, bloody stalking her. She felt as if she was about to break down mentally!

Friday 10th December '9T9'

The night before the disco had arrived. Just 24 hours stood between now and the most important day of my life at that particular time! Unfortunately for me, I was still laid up in my four-walled prison. I pleaded and pleaded with mother to let me go to the youth club that night, but she was having none of it. She said that if I couldn't go to school with my gammy leg, then I couldn't go to the youth club, that I would have to wait patiently until the disco. Christ she was so annoying and strict! Gemma, Jay, and Rick, on the other hand, did go. (lucky buggers)

Honestly, I was going insane! Being stuck inside the house was torturous! I was talking to myself, and I swear I heard someone say something back one particular time, bloody crapped myself! I was wandering the house endlessly, regularly clock watching and I even counted every single brick that was on the outside wall of our house, so yeah, bored was an understatement!

So, back to Gemma, Jay, and Rick. Rick and Jay had spent the evening playing football, oh, and I nearly forgot to mention, Rick had only gone and asked Zoe to be his date for the disco! I honestly didn't see that one coming. I didn't even know he fancied Zoe. He most certainly had kept that one quiet! Jay, as usual, was going solo as he did every year, his plan never seemed to fail, he always ended up with someone by the end of the night.

Gemma and Zoe just chilled out, sitting on the chairs on the side of the indoor sports area watching the guys play football. Grace then came along and requested a private chat with Gemma.

Gemma told me that she did seem pretty upset about something, so she agreed.

Grace and Gemma made their way through to the quiet lounge where they could have a chat without any ears around. There weren't many people there that night which was nothing unusual as the day before the discos were usually pretty dead.

As soon as Grace sat down she started to sob which made Gemma very worried, she sat down next to her, put her arm around her shoulder and asked Grace what was wrong. Once Grace had composed herself she went on to tell Gemma that she had been kicked out of the house by her drunken mother. Grace had then apparently walked to her dad's house, that he told her to "Piss off" then chased her down the street with a butcher knife!

Well, Gemma was in shock! She didn't know what to say other than did she call the police and where was she going to go? Grace told Gemma that she would be staying at her sister's house but just needed to be able to vent to someone about what happened before she went! Gemma assured her and advised that she would be better off not going back home, to stay with her sister until it all blew over and told her that she was worth much more and did not deserve to be treated like that.

Grace seemed happy that she could count on Gemma and that she could trust her. Grace then asked how things were getting on with her, Gemma just sighed and looked to the floor. She told Grace that her parents were still fighting, that she was looking forward to the disco with me and explained what had happened with Franko two evenings prior.

For some reason Grace seemed highly interested in the latter two, she seemed to want to know a lot of details about Gemma and me, wanting to know what exactly what Franko had said to Gemma and how she felt about him.

Am I paranoid here? But why did she need to know all that, what was she after? I remember thinking.

For some reason, I didn't like her! She seemed genuine but something inside was telling me that she was no good, she literally made me shudder, god only knows what it was, intuition maybe? Or was it because I wasn't letting go of that dirty look she gave me!

So after a lengthy conversation Grace left to go to her sister's house (apparently) look, there I go again, doubting her every move! Gemma rejoined Zoe to watch the lads play football for the rest of the evening until it was time to go home.

Saturday 11th December '2121'

It was here! That day had arrived! The day that would define my life for years to come! It was disco night, and I was buzzing! Oh, and guess what? I was finally allowed out of my pit and by god I was going to make the most of it! We caught a lift to the disco with Graham's dad.

Graham had stolen some beers from his dad's fridge and was sneakily passing them around between Jay, Rick and myself, cheers dude! To my satisfaction, Graham's dad was embarrassing Graham by telling him not to get caught masturbating in the girl's toilets, as it would be the closest he would get to some so-called 'gash' that night!

Sensibly, I asked Graham's dad a series of questions, for example, how many girls had Graham slept with? I only asked because 'apparently' Graham's dad regularly hooked him up with young college girls from his nightclub that he owned. Well, Graham just turned and looked at me with piercing eyes, my god if looks could kill! It was hilarious! Graham's dad just chuckled to himself, and without hesitation, informed us that Graham most certainly DID NOT hook up with girls from his club!
Ha! Brilliant, another lie caught out, he was certainly going through a string of bad luck, karma's such a bitch!

We had arrived at the disco. We got out of the car, all smiles and ready for the night ahead. Well, apart from Graham who's facial expression looked like he had just gone through a colonoscopy procedure, he was not happy that he had been caught out once more! We made our way inside and signed in, and the atmosphere was electric! So many people had turned up, the place was packed!

I could hear the music pumping from a distance over the countless of conversations that groups and groups of people were having around me.

My first port of call was to look for Gemma. I had been eagerly but nervously waiting to see her all day. I had not seen her since the previous Tuesday evening. I was missing her. I could only describe the feeling as if my left arm was missing from my body. It just proved to me though of how much I cared for her.

I looked around the building and couldn't find her, so I got my phone out to text her. Oh my god, how awkward were those phones back then to text, I remember we had to press a single button 3 or 4 times, to get ONE letter, it was so frustrating, and this was even before predictive text existed so if you buggered up, you had to start again! A bit like those old flaming rotary dial phones, they were the worst ever! Especially if you messed up the very last number because you had to hang up the phone and start again! It almost caused an anxiety attack trying to dial those last few numbers!

Anyway, I had texted Gemma from my 'brick' and awaited a reply, and surprisingly she texted back within a few moments, she was outside waiting for me. Then I remembered! I had told her I would wait for her outside! Oh crap, how could I forget that! I thought.

I made my way back through the crowds of people and went outside to greet her.

There she was, I froze to the spot in amazement as she looked stunning! She wore a silky purple dress, her hair in a loose perm and make-up to perfection!

I still get goosebumps, even now as I write this! I couldn't believe that a girl as amazing as she would go for some blonde, curtain-haired boy like me! Gemma turned around and saw me stood there with the biggest and broadest smile on my face.

"There you are!" said Gemma,

"Hey, oh you look beautiful, absolutely stunning!" I replied,

"Aw thanks, Mike" she replied.

Gemma hugged me, I hugged her back, she also smelt terrific! Her perfume was like a natural coconutty smell, and it wasn't an overwhelming smell either, it was just right, not like some of those sprays that give you an asthma attack when you got too near, then got stuck in your nostril hair causing it to linger for days after!

We linked arms and made our way inside, through the busy crowds and into the dance hall where Jay, a mardy looking Graham, Rick, and Zoe were sat. We joined up another table and sat down next to them, all buzzing and ready to party.

The DJ was playing all the latest songs from that era, looking back on them though they were so cheesy! They got you in such a hyper mood! Come on, who doesn't like a bit of 90's cheesy pop music?!

As the night progressed, I became knackered from all the dancing with Gemma, Jay, Rick, and Zoe. I needed to sit down to have a breather. The sweat was literally pouring from my face as I slouched on my chair. Jay came and sat down with me, both of us equally as exhausted.

"So how are you both getting on mate?" Jay asked,

   "Ah brilliant thanks, things couldn't be going any better" I replied,

   "Cool, cool, so when are ya gonna ask her out?" Jay asked,

   "Chill Jay, its all in hand, I'll do it later" I replied,

Well at that, what song came on next? Only that famous song from 1997 that had numbers as a title! What a tune! I still remember the dance moves even to this day! This song also happened to be Gemma's favourite, and I could see on her face what was to come next, yep! She came bounding over to Jay and myself then just dragged us back up on the dance floor!

As I was being dragged back to the dance floor, I turned and asked Graham (who still had his dummy thrown out of the pram by the way) if he wanted to join us?

   "No that's just gay" he replied.

Bugger it, forget about that 'tantrumming toddler!' If he wasn't going to enjoy himself then I'm certainly going to I thought, it was only because no one would have him as their date for the evening, but I didn't care I was having fun, confidently dancing to the moves of the song!

After a fun few hours the last song came on, and to no surprise, it was a slow dance, right here we go, now is the time, it's now, or never I thought to myself.

I took Gemma's hand and led her to the dance floor. We faced each other, I put my hands on her hips, she put her arms around the back of my neck, and we began to sway and dance, circulating around and around slowly. It was our first slow dance together and honestly, I could have lived in that moment for all eternity, it felt amazing it was such a special moment.

I spent quite a lot of time living in that moment, taking mental notes from the atmosphere around me, the feel of her silky dress over her hips, the sensation of her warm breath on my neck. I whispered into her ear,

"Gemma?"

Gemma looked into my eyes, I looked back into hers, both of us fixated into that moment of time, it was all so serious, like we both desperately wanted this to last forever.

"Will you go out with me?" I asked,

"Yes!" she replied,

We both stood still for a moment, gazed into each other's eyes. Gemma then leaned in slowly and began to kiss me. My whole body tingled with love and pride, I had never felt so much love and happiness in an instant like that before.

Before we knew it, the song was over. The night was over. The lights came back on while we were still kissing and the only thing that broke it was the sound of Jay, Rick, and Zoe cheering and jeering, which did make us laugh!

We both cuddled each other tightly, then made our way out of the dance hall, through the crowds of people and outside to await our lifts home, and it was freezing! Coming from a nice, warm building then into the freezing outdoors, it certainly sent a shock through our bodies. Gemma cuddled up to me in an attempt to warm up so I put my coat around her so she wouldn't get cold.

Out the corner of my right eye, I saw something charge at me. Before I could even react, an extremely painful, bone crushing pain pulsated from the right-hand side of my face! I fell to the floor hard! I couldn't see properly, everything was a blur!

All I could hear was Gemma screaming out with fear and lots of people shouting. As I tried to stand back up, another severe, hard impact struck my ribs! I couldn't breathe. Gasping for air I fell to the floor once more, as I looked up I could just make out a persons face, I could see a scar, I could hear his deep, frightening voice raging at me, it was Franko!

I could vaguely see Jay, Graham, and Rick trying to hold him back. I then heard a loud cracking sound, like something heavy smashing onto a bone and before I knew it, I was being dragged inside the youth club by Rick and Jay.
Once inside I heard someone bolt the door shut. Gemma sat down next to me, and she was in a hysteria of emotion, I could see her mascara pouring down her face due to her tears.

"Mike, stay still! Your bleeding" Jay said,

I could hear the tremble in his voice as he spoke. He held a damp cloth over the cut on my face to numb the pain, also to try and stop it bleeding.

Still, in a daze from the impact to my face, I asked,

"What the fuck happened?"

"Fucking Franko mate, don't worry, I hit him with a brick, he won't be getting up anytime soon!" Replied Jay.

As soon as he had said that, there was a loud, heavy, banging noise that pounded on the door! The shouting from outside had resumed. I couldn't hear what exactly what Franko was saying, I could, however, hear my name mentioned, Gemma's name and the words "gonna die" and "get you."

Franko had gone psychopathic! He had lost it! He repeatedly kicked and threw his body into the door in a desperate attempt to finish the job. Suddenly it all stopped, there was no noise. By this time my vision had mostly returned. I looked around the hall, and everyone was silent, all with a look of terror in their eyes.

SMASH!

A brick then was launched through one of the windows! Everyone screamed and ran into the dance hall apart from Gemma, Jay and myself, Gemma cowered over me, and I held her tightly, both of us frightened out our wits! Then the most fantastic sound rang out loud from outside, the sound of sirens and the screeching of tires.

"Get on the floor now" I heard a muffled voice say from outside,

"Get off me, get off me" I heard Franko shouting.

I heard a car door slam shut then it all fell silent once more, so quiet you could hear a pin drop on the floor. It was over, finally over! Gemma was so overwhelmed by it all, bless her, crying her poor heart out. She tried to get her words out but just couldn't. I had tears welling up as well. It hurt so much to see her so upset, even more than the throbbing pain from my face and ribs. I just hugged her so tightly, desperately trying to reassure her that everything would be okay.

As she calmed down a little I pulled away, I could see the fresh blood from my face soaked into her hair from where my face must have been laying. I must have looked like a train crash victim.

"Mike, I'm sorry, so so sorry!" Sobbed Gemma,

"It's not your fault babe, he's a prick" I replied,

"But if we weren't together this wouldn't have happened" replied Gemma,

"Listen, babe, I didn't see it coming and nothing, I mean nothing is going to break us! I have wanted this for so long" I replied.

Her sobbing turned into full-blown crying, and she hugged me tightly once more.

I meant what I said to her! I was going to fight for us to stay together, to the death if I must! No-one, not even that dickhead was going to ruin what we had.

I had gone through so much to get where I was that day, I wasn't going to bow out without a fight.

The police then came in a few minutes later to take statements and to reassure everyone that the situation had been resolved, that we were safe. Unfortunately, I needed to go to the hospital for stitches as my cut was too deep to heal on its own.

Friday 31st December '9T9'

Nearly three weeks had passed since the disco, and during that time I was a nervous wreck! I had kept a strong face to Gemma and the others, but inside I was falling apart, like a tornado ripping up the beautiful landscape. I was still waking up screaming with terror in the night. I had to take beta blockers which were prescribed by my doctor before I left the house so that I didn't have an anxiety attack while I was out.

I had finally found out more information about what happened that night. The events unfolded so quickly that my brain had blocked most of the trauma out, it was just the damn flashbacks that got to me while I was awake. Franko had hit me while wearing a knuckle duster! No wonder it had hurt so bloody much, I thought to myself! I had to spend 24 hours in the hospital as I had suffered a severe concussion. They did several tests on me to make sure that I didn't have any swelling or a bleed on the brain, but all was okay. Gemma, bless her stayed with me the entire time.

The police had suggested that we all took leave from school until the new term started, which as you could imagine was highly satisfying! Franko was arrested (obviously) and given a restraining order, so if the twat came anywhere near us, he'd be going away! He was also awaiting a court date so with a bit of luck we could have sued the arse off him. The only thing that still puzzled me was how did Franko know we were there? And how did he know precisely when we were coming out? Someone must have tipped him off but who the hell was it?

Christmas Day, well what a fantastic day that was! I received a load of new CD's, DVD's, clothes, a new hi-fi system, oh! And socks from my Gran (thanks Gran, really needed those!)

The greatest present of all was a surprise visit from Gemma. The mother and Gemma's mum secretly organized for us to see each other in the afternoon! It was so lovely to see her as we had only spoken on the phone since the disco night, only because both sets of parents were too paranoid to let us out just in case of shit hitting the fan again, so, unfortunately, phone calls had to do.

It was so frustrating as there was no such thing as Skype, face time and other social media back then, so it was tough to stay in touch, especially if you wanted to keep the conversation private. We used to make up keywords for what we meant, It was so funny thinking and looking back at it though!

Anyway, she came over for Christmas Dinner and spent the evening with us, which ended up being so awkward, thanks to my bloody younger sister who was just sat staring and smiling at Gemma all evening! She was so bloody creepy. I swear something was missing in that brain of hers!

Now! That leads me to New Year's Eve 1999! The millennium! The night before all the computers were going to crash all over the world (Yeah right! I can't believe we all believed that crap!)

The parents had cautiously let us go out to Jay's parent's pub for the evening to celebrate the new year. Come on it wasn't just like any other New Years Eve, it was the millennium, Y2K! A night to remember – for all the wrong reasons in my case!

Jay, Graham, Rick and I had snook out of Jay's parent's pub. It was so boring! It was full of old people blabbering on about how bad our generation was, (Ahem! We could all hear them!)

The old men moaning about how their wives never let them out and always questioned everything they did, that they were never satisfied with anything they did around the house, I remember thinking, is this what it's going to be like when I'm all old and married? Flaming off-putting that was!
We couldn't take it any longer, not how we wanted to spend the night.

So, with me still carrying a black eye and a stitched up scab near my temple we went out and wandered the streets. Graham, unfortunately, was in perfect form! I swear he was about to give me a heart attack! He somehow, I don't know how, managed to convince us all to go and wind up Paedo Paul.

Paedo Paul was this really strange, I mean, really strange person. He regularly used to sit outside our school and wave to us as we left on the bus. Although in his 40's Paul still lived with his parents and did a paper round. He dressed weird too! Like in trousers that were too short for him, a shirt and blazer with a pink baseball cap? Odd, very odd indeed!

One of Graham's 'hobbies' was to wind him up and get him to chase him down the street, cruel, so cruel!

This night, Graham somehow had got hold of a load of fireworks and being the very immature teenager's Graham, Rick and Jay were, lit the rockets, in their bare hands I add! Then started throwing them around before they exploded! Throwing them onto the road and into people's gardens, what complete idiots!

Me, being the mature one of the bunch tried and tried to advise
them of the dangers from letting off fireworks in one's hand,
throwing them and allowing them to explode not too far away
from us, but all I got called was a boring lightweight and
Corporal Skid Risk? Who the hell is Corporal Skid Risk?

So, with just two rockets left we arrived at Paedo Paul's house.
I was dreading as to what Graham was going to do next!

To my absolute horror, he pushed the damn rocket as far as he
could into the ground, right underneath Paul's lounge window,
lit it, then legged it along with Jay and Rick!

What the hell? I just froze, not knowing what to do until it
exploded while still lodged into the ground! Paul's dad
immediately looked out the window and saw me! Yes, Just me
stood there with a horrified look on my face, well that was it! I
ran, ran so fast that I quickly caught up with Jay, Rick and
Graham! After a few hundred yards of sprinting, we hid behind
a hedge along the side street,

   "Jasmine, you fucking prick, what did you do that for?" I
shouted,

   "Oh shut up and have some fun!" replied Graham,

   "Fun? You call that bloody fun! We'll be locked up!" I
replied,

   "Nah, done this plenty of times mate, watch this!"

At that Graham lit the last rocket, right under my fucking nose,
so much I felt my nose hair singe! He lobbed it over the hedge,
and what did it land on?

The bonnet of a fucking police car!

"FUCKING RUN!" Jay shouted!

Well, we just split and legged it as fast as we could, all of going off in different directions. I didn't look back, but I certainly heard the explosion from the rocket! I hurdled over the nearest hedge, landed on my arse in someone's garden, got up, ran to the gate and climbed over it as fast as I could, then sprinted into the random person garden.

I struggled with my asthma which was set off by a combination of running too fast and panic, so I stayed there for a few moments to catch my breath. I then heard sirens, lots of sirens in the distance.

"fuck, I have got to get out of here" I thought, I crept through the hedge at the bottom of the garden, bloody painful that was! I certainly didn't anticipate how prickly it would be.

As I got through the hedge with tens of prickles lodged in my body I reached the road, I looked left and then right. I could see Jay's parent's pub just a hundred yards or so to my right, but before I could make a run for it, I quickly had to back up into the hedge as a police riot van was coming, traveling down the road at high speed in my direction.

I backed up just enough so the police wouldn't see me and got prickled again, right on my arse that time, urgh, so uncomfortable, I swear some of them actually got lodged into my buttocks that time!

It was then that I began to question my life in general, like what the hell am I doing hanging around with that lot? I'm going to end up in prison and getting banged by desperate inmates, no thank you and Graham, I'm gonna to kill him when I see him, I thought!

The police van then came screaming by me at high speed, went passed me then turned left down the road where we were to begin with. I was safe. It had gone. I peered out of the hedge once more, looked left, then right and what did I see in the distance? Bloody Graham, Jay, and Rick scampering across the road and into the car park of Jay's pub.
The bastards, I thought to myself, I was so angry with them!

I couldn't hear any more traffic, so I legged it across the road, onto the footpath and just sprinted along the path like Usain Bolt. All of the time panicking that I was going to get caught as I was in the open with nothing to hide behind. With just adrenaline powering my body, I got closer and closer and didn't stop until I reached the pub.

Thankfully, with no other drama's I had made it. I jogged around the side of the building then into the car park, where Jay greeted me, along with Rick and Graham, all happy, laughing and joking about what just happened.

"Ya didn't get caught then?" said Graham,

"You're a fucking arsehole" I struggled to say while trying to catch my breath,

"Ah come on mate, it was funny!" said Rick,

"For you morons maybe, seriously, why do I hang around with you bell-ends?" I said,

"Cos you'll have no one else to hang around with!" Jay replied sarcastically,

"Bugger off" I replied.

We heard the sound of sirens once more so we quickly figured that the best thing we could do was to go inside, go upstairs and on Jay's computer games, well they did! I intended to make a slight detour to the toilet in an attempt to get some of those prickles out of my arse cheeks.

In Jay's bathroom, I was loudly Umming and arring, desperately trying to get those thorns out with tweezers! Finally, I had succeeded, I had got them all! Twenty minutes it took me to get all of those prickles out!

I flushed the toilet as that's where I put all the thorns and then emerged from the bathroom all red-faced and sweaty, only to be greeted by those three prunes just staring at me looking all puzzled and shocked,

"What?" I asked inquisitively,

"Were you wanking in my toilet?" replied Jay with a serious tone,

"Don't be so stupid Jay, why would I do that?" I replied,

To get them to believe I wasn't masturbating in Jay's toilet I had to show them the gaping holes in my arse cheek from all of the thorns, well I say gaping holes I mean tiny red dots from where they were.

I had to show them as they were threatening to tell the entire school that I was caught 'tugging one off' in Jay's bathroom, the situation was embarrassing! Something I just wanted to forget quickly!

I was so wound up with them that night! I couldn't believe what Graham had done so I just spent the rest of the evening all mardy and not talking, just watching the others having fun playing on computer games and drinking bottles of lager, oh, and still taking the piss out of my apparent 'Mikey boy time in the toilet!' Certainly was not how I expected to spend my last night of the 90's.

Sunday 2nd April 2000

Just over three months had passed since that dreadful evening on New Year's Eve, thankfully, now all forgotten about! I had spent two weeks after the Christmas break being ridiculed by the entire school as Graham had gone and told everyone that I was caught masturbating in Jay's toilet, how bloody embarrassing! I even had very poor and childlike drawings of penises all over my school bag, books, and school shirts! They were arseholes, absolute arseholes!

Oh, and someone wrote, in permanent marker may I add, on the back of my white football shirt 'Cock Jerker 69!'
Still to this day I have no idea who did that, I was furious about it because it had a lot of sentimental value to it. I got that shirt when my cousin took me to watch England play in France for World Cup 98, so yeah, I was pretty angry.

Franko had been released on bail and was still awaiting a court date. His restraining order remained in place so we had seen nothing nor heard anything from him or his baboon mates since that night at the Christmas disco. Finally, things had gone back to complete normality. We were all going out again, going to the youth club, disco's and wandering the streets. It was a fantastic feeling as we didn't have to watch our backs any longer.

Gcmma and I were getting on fantastically well. We had been spending at least three evenings together a week with the gang which was fun.

Just lately though Gemma's parent's arguments had intensified quite severely, so to get away from it, Gemma had been spending a lot of time around at Zoe's or my house. It couldn't have all come at a worse time because we all had our final exams coming up, so we were all studying hard, well, apart from Graham! He just took the view that watching porn and reading porn mags somehow helped toward his Physical Education and Biology exams! I say no more on that!

Gemma and Grace had also become particularly close friends, and to be honest, she did seem pretty legit. Yes, I know what I said before, but she had actually turned out to be nice, and she had been helping Gemma get through this rough patch involving her parents. So yeah, I had taken back what I had said about her at that point. Rick and Zoe were, well, still 'kind-of' seeing each other. Nothing had progressed much between them. It seemed more like a friends with benefits type of relationship to me.

Winter was also finally over with, spring was in the air! The days had become longer and unseasonably warm over the past couple of weeks which had undoubtedly put us all in a good mood. So, with it being the last day of the weekend we had decided to go paintballing, which to my surprise was Graham's idea!

It was a massive shock to me as he wasn't usually that sophisticated as another example of his idea of 'fun' was stalking poor innocent women around town trying to get their phone numbers. Basically, he had the IQ of a horny slug! But yes, I suppose each of us has that one moment in life where we come up with a fantastic idea, and this was Graham's! However, it did come with a slight snag!

We had to walk there, which wasn't usually an issue, but it was four miles away, and it was hot, too hot.

So, after a grueling hour and a half walk in the baking sunshine, we could finally see the entrance to the paintballing place, and what a happy sight, a relief as I was knackered, we were all tired!
Zoe, Jay, and Gemma were lagging a bit so Rick, Graham and myself had slowed our pace so they could keep up! I seriously had been beginning to regret this seemingly fantastic idea Graham had.

   "This place best be open Jasmine!" I said,

   "Of course it is" Graham replied.

Graham was particularly excited about kicking our arse at paintball. Apparently, he had plenty of experience firing weapons. According to Graham, which he wouldn't shut up about all the way there was that he had a mate, someone we had not even heard of by the way, had smuggled a load of machine guns out of the Bosnian War and he and this 'friend' regularly met up and fired them at different targets in the local woodland! What a load of crap, come on if something like that had happened surely the police would have been called, and we would have read about it in the local newspaper. Like I said, an IQ of a slug.

We had arrived at the entrance of the paintballing center, finally! We just wanted to catch our breath and have a water break for a few minutes before we went in. There was a long bench at the top of the graveled driveway, so we all sat down and chilled for a while before we went in, but I noticed something down the lane, a sign with red writing on it.

I was curious as to what this was so while everyone was sat drinking water and taking a well-deserved rest I walked off to have a look.

As I got close to this sign I was able to read it, I was horrified, shocked and angry it read:

'Unfortunately due to high maintenance work, this site will be closed until July, sorry for any inconvenience caused.'

I couldn't believe it! I was fuming! I had bloody told Graham to call before we left and he said to me that he did! The lying little skunk! Right, that was it, I had enough of it, so I marched straight back to the guys. Gemma noticed the angry expression on my face as I approached them,

"Are you okay babe?" Gemma asked,

"I will be" I replied.

Calmly and kindly but gritting my teeth with rage, I asked Graham whether he had, or had not called the paintballing people to see if they were open. Confidently he confirmed that he did.

Aargh, I could feel the anger build up inside my body. With my voice still nice and calm I asked everyone to 'follow me' so we could all read this sign together.

We walked to the sign, the guys read it. While they were doing this, I was watching Graham closely with piercing eyes, channeling all my frustration through my eyes onto his lying face. As he read the sign his face dropped, he looked at me then looked at the floor. Once the others had read it, they all turned and looked at him without saying anything. I spoke out,

"I thought you called them?"

"I did" replied Graham,

"Did you heck, dude why do you lie so much?" I asked,

"I must have accidentally called another place" replied Graham,

"Jasmine, just spare us all the bullshit, and tell us the truth" I replied.

Graham admitted that he did not call the Paintballing Centre which was much to the disappointment of us all as we were looking forward to a day out. I had so many plans! Like bombarding Graham at close range with paintballs, now I just wanted to bombard him with large stones.

I take back what I said about him having an IQ of a slug! In fact, he had an IQ of a bloody pubic hair that had just fallen out of its root!

So what do we do now? What could we possibly do to make up for this? I thought, then my brain lit up like a light bulb, I knew what we could do, something we could all have fun doing, to get that much-craved adrenaline rush! Something where I could get my own back on Graham by scaring the living shit out of him!

Ghost Hunting! We could go Ghost Hunting!

My cousin John was one of those paranormal weirdo's that stalked the night looking for dead people! Perfect, I thought! I pitched my idea to the gang.

To my surprise, the guys all seemed pretty excited and up for it, even Gemma which surprised me because that sort of thing freaked her out.

I made a hasty phone call to my cousin from the nearest phone box, using the reverse charge call of course! To my delight, John was also up for it! Brilliant, finally something legit to do.

I did, however, have to beg him to come and pick us all up from the paintballing centre as there was no way I was willing to let the others walk back in that blistering heat, well apart from Graham, I didn't care for that liar at that point. But still, he picked us all up, including Graham (The shit!)

   That evening seemed to come around so slowly as we were all excited about the forthcoming event. None of us had done anything like that before so we were all psyching ourselves up and freaking each other out with different scenarios about what could happen. Some hilarious ones, like some possessed finger demon pinning Graham down and finger bashing him up the arse!
Time was drawing ever nearer to John picking us up.

I had spent the last half an hour telling the guy's ghost stories that John had told me, like when John went to this old mental asylum and started intimidating an evil ghoul and then felt something strangle him with unseen hands!

Graham was freaked out by the thought of this happening. Ha! Brilliant, I remember thinking, and that now some much needed payback was to hopefully happen that night.

John turned up 10 minutes late. I was freaking out! I hate people being late for something! It all just ends up with everything being a massive rush which set my anxiety and OCD off!

We all plunged into the car, excitingly talking about the freaky things that may happen. I got into the front of the car to sit next to John, and we set off. After we had all quietened down the anticipation was over. John revealed to us where our destination lie! The Abandoned Asylum, one of the most haunted locations in the area! Oh my god, this was going to be amazing I thought. I had heard so many stories of what had gone off there like patients being mistreated and apparently, it was haunted by a furious demon type of thing!

After an hours drive, we had arrived. Stood in front of us was a very large, derelict, spooky building. The sun was setting behind it which gave the building a dark silhouette look. Everything was very still and quiet, too quiet! A shiver went shooting down my spine!

As we walked toward the building, my nerves began to set in. I couldn't figure out whether it was fear or excitement, or both? Gemma clung onto my arm and reiterated to me how frightened she was. I assured her that it would all be okay and nothing bad was going to happen, that we were only going to go inside, look around, scare the crap out of Graham and then go home.

We had got to the door, I looked around and could see all the dark paneless windows, there were hundreds of them! All exposed to the elements.

We walked through the door without hesitation. It was dark, very dark! The only bit of light that we could see was from the fading sunlight through some of the windows.

Fortunately, John had brought torches so he handed them to us one by one. Initially we struggled to feel for the switches but we managed to turn them. Now we could see where the hell we were going.

The paint on the walls were all peeling off, vegetation had begun to grow up the walls of the long and dark corridors, and the odd bit of graffiti sprayed onto the walls certainly added to the atmosphere.

It was so quiet apart from the sudden crack of fallen glass and wood that we trampled over. John stopped us, he turned around and whispered to us that we were to be going down into the tunnels, oh my, that did it for me, I was freaked out! No one mentioned bloody tunnels! I tried to reassure myself that it couldn't be that bad as if it was, John certainly wouldn't be going back there.

John lived on a caravan site with his wife, Sara. He was quite a bit older than me, 24 at the time. John had quite the reputation of being a bit of a hard man. He certainly did look rough especially with his shaved head, however, he had settled quite a bit over the years, even still, I wouldn't want to piss him off!

We walked down the iron staircase and into the dark, narrow bowels of the asylum. Gemma, bless her, couldn't go any further as she was too terrified, so John agreed to stay where we were and do a bit of calling out. I tried to lighten the fearful mood a little by reminding Graham that it was time for the finger demon to appear but the others just sniggered nervously.

It went quiet, uncomfortably quiet.

John quietly asked us to turn our torches off, we reluctantly agreed. After a few moments of silence, John broke that silence and called out in a deep voice which made us shudder,

"If there is anyone there, please let yourselves be known!"

Oh crap, please, please don't do anything I thought. Gemma clung onto me even tighter and buried her head in my chest, but nothing happened. John persisted with the calling out until something weird happened. There was a bang, a bang from the darkness of the tunnel, well we shat ourselves (Not literally) but stayed stood still.

"Thank you, could you do that again please?" asked John.

Another bang seemed to follow his question. I was trying to think logically, it could just be wind? A vent, or even an infected plague-ridden rodent! Until John asked it to bang twice and it bloody did! Well, I freaked!

Fuck this I thought! All of us apart from John huddled together and what did Graham do? stupidly he said:

"Come on you coward to something proper!"

"What the fuck did you say that for? Do you want us to die?" I immediately replied.

Well, that was it, there was a loud dragging sound, which sounded like a large piece of furniture, loudly being scraped across the floor!

Fuck that! We just screamed out loudly and ran back up the iron staircase, then ran as fast as we could down the dark corridor. Somehow Gemma managed to keep hold of my hand while we were running, it certainly didn't take long to reach the exit and then back to the car without looking back.

John opened the car us while laughing to himself, what the hell was he bloody laughing at? We could have died at the hands of a mental patient Demon thing. We all got in, frightened out of our wits, John then got in the front still proudly chuckling to himself.

"What the hell was that?" I asked,

"Ha! It's normal mate." Replied John,

"Normal? You call that normal? It's not going to follow us is it?" I asked,

"Don't say that Mike!" said Gemma,

"No mate, course it won't!" Replied John,

"Can we just get out of here please?" Asked Gemma fearfully.

John turned on the car engine and drove away. Thank god that was over! My plan had epically failed. So instead of scaring Graham, Graham had only gone and pissed off this Demon thing which scared the crap out of us all. Certainly something I wouldn't be doing again anytime soon, but on the positive side, It was something ticked off from my bucket list and that I now believe in demons, spirits, ghouls or whatever you call them!

Monday 3rd April 2000

Monday 3rd April 2000 went down as one of the most bizarre and strangest days of my life. I swear it had something to do with that ghost hunting thing we did the night beforehand, like some Demon that liked to embarrass you in front of everyone had possessed me with all of its might! I called my jinx day, a day where everything that could go wrong, went wrong so here we go, this is what happened,

Gemma and I were laying down on a blanket in a grass field on a hilltop watching the sunset. We had been there many hours, spending time together, laughing, joking and enjoying some rare alone time together, away from our friends, parents, and exams.

It had been a beautiful warm day without a cloud in sight. It even had a gentle breeze to keep us at the right temperature. It was perfect. As the sun was just about to disappear behind the distant hill Gemma looked at me and smiled, I looked at her and smiled back. I still couldn't believe that I had such a fantastic girlfriend, things were so perfect!

Things were about to get even better when, finally after nearly four months of going out she said to me,

   "Mike, I love you!"

Oh my god, my heart melted! I had wanted to tell her that for weeks but didn't want to freak her out, so it was amazing to hear her say it first.

   "Oh babe, I love you too" I immediately replied.

We then began to kiss. I could taste her strawberry lip balm which I tasted lush! Seriously if that stuff were edible I would have it with every meal, it was so nice!

Suddenly, out of nowhere, it began to pour down with rain, like a sudden monsoon! Like someone had thrown a bucket of water over us.

I quickly pulled the blanket from under us and put it over the top of our heads in an attempt to keep us dry, but the rain suddenly stopped.

That was weird, I thought, I swear there weren't even any clouds around!

I took the blanket off my head so I could look around, but there was no one there, where the hell had Gemma gone? There was no solid object for miles around for her to hide behind so where on earth was she?

Suddenly there was a woman's voice, an erotic tone of voice,

   "You're late Mike, you naughty boy"

I turned round to see who this was that spoke so passionately.

To my absolute horror, it was my mother! Dressed in a Betty Boo costume!

I yelped out loud and got up from the ground very quickly, I was confused,

   "Mother what the actual fuck?" I shouted.

She was just stood there looking at me like she wanted to pounce on me and eat me like I was some sort-of steak! So fucking gross!

This can't be real surely? I closed my eyes. I reopened them moments later, and Gemma appeared in front of me, I looked around, mother had gone!

"Are you okay Mike?" she asked,

"I think I have hit my head on something" I replied still perplexed about what had just happened,

"What do you mean babe?" Gemma asked,

"Fucking mother! No, it doesn't matter! Gross, so gross!" I replied.

All of a sudden it began to rain heavily again and I just froze to the spot, getting soaked very quickly.

In an instant, like at a click of a finger I was in my bedroom looking up at my ceiling, What the hell was going on? I thought. It was like I had teleported. I felt all wet! What the fuck is happening? I asked myself.

I looked down, I was soaked with water as was my bed sheets and pillow, god I hope I haven't urinated in my bed, I thought, I was so confused.

Suddenly mother came into my bedroom and shouted,

"Michael Miller, get up! You are going to be late for school!"

Well, I shot up out of bed quickly looking at her for fear of what she was going to do to me.

She just glared at me, looked down then turned her head away and started laughing to herself.

"What's so funny?" I asked.

Still turned away she pointed to my lower regions, I looked down, I couldn't believe it! I had an erection! So clearly you could see it through my tight boxer shorts!

"Get out, get out now!" I shouted,

"You got it soldier boy" she replied.

Laughing to herself as she left the room, how bloody embarrassing was that?
Little did I know at the time that the day was going to get a whole lot worse!

So, after half an hour of trying to 'de-erect' myself using cold water from a tap, I had killed it! I Almost missed the bus because of it!
I went on to losing my footing as I got off the school bus, ended up smacking my coccyx on the bottom step (Which was bloody painful by the way, don't try it!) I had made it to school in one piece (just).

After form time it was our first lesson of the day, science. I used to enjoy science until the teachers banned the whole year from doing experiments because of some little idiot that thought it would be funny to put acid into the tropical fish tank which killed the poor things. They never found out who did it, however, I did have my suspicions!

During the lesson I was not with it, I couldn't stop thinking about that vivid dream that I had, which certainly turned out to be my worst nightmare, still makes me shudder to this day with what bloody mother did. Anyway, enough of her, I was thinking about the feelings that I had felt when Gemma told me that she loved me. Obviously, that was not real. However, it had put things into perspective for me. We really needed to have more alone time together, away from our mates, away from parents and definitely away from all the revision.

As I was completely distracted by all of those thoughts, the teacher certainly noticed that I was away with the fairies. Apparently, he called my name out twice, but I didn't hear him. I must have been in so much of a daydream even to notice him talking or also saying my name.

So, he snapped me out of my daydream in a way that he was most famous for, getting a metal ruler and slamming it hard onto the wooden table I was sat behind, oh my god it scared the crap out of me! It made my bloody ears ring.

   "Miller, what was I just talking about?" the teacher said in a firm voice.

Still in a dreamy state and not quite being able to grasp the difference between reality and my subconscious mind I replied with the words,

   "Grass field sir?"

Well, he just looked at me all gone out, he looked very confused himself! I could hear the rest of the class sniggering away in the background.

Graham, who sat next to me whispered,

"What the fuck is the grass field?"

I just ignored him, staring at the teacher wondering what he was going to do next.

"Miller, stand up and come to the front of the class now!" He said.

Okay, now I was worried, what the hell was he going to do? I had no choice but to stand up and go to the front of the class. The teacher then walked over to my table and sat down in my seat leaving me stood there looking like an idiot. The silence from everyone was just awkward, especially as they were all looking at me.

"So Miller, please educate us?" said the teacher,

"What about sir?" I replied,

"About what I was talking about, and what this business is about the grass field?" he replied.

Well, I just stood there in silence, I didn't know what to say! I most certainly was not going to tell him about the grass field thing. I would never live it down!

"Sir, can I ask Mike a question please?" asked Graham,

"If you must Gullard, as long as it's nothing obscene" replied the teacher,

"Mike, what is that on your shoulder?" Graham asked.

I looked down at my left shoulder. I couldn't believe what I saw!

"Oh shit!" I exclaimed,

"Literally" chuckled Graham.

I had a massive dollop of bird poo on my school shirt, unbelievable! I thought, and what the hell had that thing been eating? It didn't look right! It was like mayonnaise mixed with curry sauce, totally disgusting!

To my relief, the school's horn rang out loudly, my damn saviour! However, the cringing drone sound gave the shudders, the same feeling of when a fork it scraped across a plate. It was the end of class, thank god!
My first mission was to gather my things, then rush to the toilets to get that thing washed off, and of course, Graham just had to follow me to the toilet didn't he!.

In the toilets, I was desperately trying to scrub my shirt clean with tears in my eyes from all the gagging and retching. Graham, not helping whatsoever, just laughing away at my misfortune! Why the hell has this happened to me? No, seriously what have I done that's so wrong in this world to deserve this? I thought, Wait! Just wait a minute, this was Graham's fault! He's the one that intimidated that Demon thing!

"Graham this is your fault!" I yelled,

"Why is this my fault?" he replied,

"You! Intimidating that bloody creature last night, you've jinxed me!" I shouted,

"What the fuck Mike, it's only a bit of shit" he replied while giggling away to himself, the twat!

I was so angry at the situation! If he only knew half of what had been happening that day, then he would have understood, saying that, this was Graham we were talking about, so no, he wouldn't have.

Finally! I had got the 'poop' out. However, there was still a bright stain on my shirt and guess what? I didn't bring a jumper with me, so I had to walk around all day with everyone seeing this yellowy stain on my shirt, great, just great I thought!

The rest of the day was pretty uneventful, UNTIL, yes until assembly! What a horrible experience! Not only was Graham farting throughout, and the smell, oh my god the smell! It nearly killed me! It was that bad the aroma could have stripped all of the paint from the walls. It was that bad! And guess what? The teachers thought it was me! So yet again, I had to stand up in front of everyone, the whole school that time! Thanks, Graham, now everyone thought that it was me that produced such a horrific stench.

Following that grueling experience and for what remained of the school day, on the bus ride home, no one sat near me. No one came near me. It was like I was going to give them radiation poisoning or something, this was much to the amusement of Jay, Rick, and Graham, and did they stick up for me and tell everyone what had actually happened? No, no they didn't, the arseholes!

Friday 7th April 2000

Friday couldn't have rolled around quick enough. Thankfully my 'jinx day' had ended entirely on Monday. However, the rest of the week was humiliating. Passing comments about my bowel motions and bird poo on my shirt was a hot topic!

My new nickname was 'Swallow' yes, swallow! Very bloody original, I mean what the hell has a Swallow got to do with anything? Yes, it's a bird but that's it, so, so very immature!

What I was really looking forward to though was a long overdue date night with Gemma. Both of us had been so eager to get out, just the two of us. Don't get me wrong it was fantastic being around the others, well, apart from Graham but it was just so lovely to have some alone time finally. We had decided to go bowling.
Unfortunately for me though, I was harboring a stinking cold! All day I had been sneezing loudly and I had a barky cough to go with it. I seriously thought I was coming down with Ebola or something!

We arrived at the Bowling Alley via a generous, but awkward lift from mother, with that 'boner' incident still fresh in my mind I didn't want to talk to her because hearing that voice made me cringe, I kept asking myself if I was going through some sort-of Post Traumatic stress which I hoped would fade away in time. What didn't help though was that every time we passed each other at home, she would snigger to herself! The stupid moo!

After Gemma said thank you and goodbye to mother for the lift, we made our way inside. It was a bright, mild evening, so we were both wearing casual summer clothing. While waiting for our bowling shoes Gemma asked me if everything was okay between mother and I.

I just came up with an excuse about us having a war of words over revision and that we still had not made up from it. I certainly was not going to tell her the real reason as that would have been just too awkward. Gemma and I had not talked about things that intimate, we were close, but not that close! We still had not even mentioned the 'love' word to one and other as of yet, however, I certainly did love her but was waiting for the right time to tell her. I was 99.9% sure she felt the same way, but as always, there was teeny tiny niggling doubt in my mind!

For some reason, I was slightly nervous about bowling. I think it was because I had not played for years and I think the man syndrome had kicked in! Meaning that I wanted to show off my bowling skills to her but was scared of the ball sticking in my fingers then end up smashing a light on the ceiling or something. Gemma, on the other hand, was somewhat confident and was already putting her shoes on and already making her way toward the lanes.

I, on the other hand, was too busy smelling the shoes before hesitantly inserting my feet into a rather sticky and smelly pair of shoes, certain that they squelched as I walked to meet Gemma at the chosen lane.

"Hey babe, you okay? You look stressed." Gemma asked inquisitively,

"Hey, yeah I'm fine it's just my shoes stink! Not because of me! I think someone forgot to wash for a week before wearing them and now they have given them to me!" I replied.

Gemma bust out with laughter while looking down at my feet,

"You must be the unlucky one as mine feel brand new!" She replied through her laughter,

"Do you want to bowl first? Or shall I with my 'clean' shoes!" She continued,

"You go ahead. I feel that I may slide all over with these things on my feet" I replied.

I felt all overcome with nerves, not because of the shoes but because of my overactive mind. I was hoping I didn't mess things up tonight, show myself up and slide down the lane, drop the ball on my foot or even worse – lose!

Gemma stepped up to take the first bowl, and bowled that ball down the lane with perfection.

"Strike ha-ha! Your turn! Good luck!" said a confident and cheerful Gemma.
I couldn't believe it! I certainly had a game on my hands, so I took a deep breath, calmed my nerves, picked up a bowling ball, secretly hoping the holes weren't full with someone else's sweat or food, ugh, thinking of that now makes my stomach churn.

"Okay, here goes!"

I stepped up, lined the ball up, and...

I threw it, I literally, threw it! The noise it made as it slammed down on the alley echoed as it hit the lane causing other people to look over at us!

   "Oops, soorrryy" I meekly said to everyone.

I was blushing. I felt my face turn red. I felt hot, like my head was in an oven, and at that moment I wished it was!

Gemma, on the other hand, was laughing so hard I could not make out what she was trying to say. I just stood there with a confused and dim look on my face that seemed to provoke her to laugh harder.

All of this was interrupted when a goofy looking worker approached us to make sure that we had caused no damage, and asked if we would like the side rails putting up, similar to that of kids, I declined. He then further embarrassed me by showing me how I should bowl, Gemma and I exchanged several glances throughout his demonstration. I felt relieved when he left, as did Gemma.

   "My Dad bowls better than that" Chuckled Gemma,

   "Mine doesn't bowl at all, that's where the problem lies!" I replied.

We continued our game with no more issues apart from the fact that at the end of the game I lost!

Gemma was so happy about this! She turned out to be as competitive as I was, I liked this side of her.

We headed for the bar to grab some snacks and soft drinks. The conversation then became a bit more of a serious one,

"I never used to laugh like this with Franko! We never did this either, the bowling I mean, not the eating."

Gemma said while trying to keep the conversation light-hearted.

I was a bit taken aback by her statement, not particularly sure how to reply. Franko was still a touchy subject for me with what he had done. It was something I was desperately trying to forget.

"We can do this whenever you want to" I replied,

"I'd like to do it again, you're really funny even when you are not trying to be, like when you just stood there staring at me after you threw that ball onto the lane!" replied Gemma,

"As if it was my fault?" I said jokingly,

"No it wasn't your fault, it was the balls!" Gemma chuckled,

"All that sweat in the holes caused me to lose grip! And I was looking at you because you were trying to say something or I thought you were!" I replied,

"Er yeah! I was saying, stop looking at me you're making me laugh!" She chuckled,

"Oh, right I didn't catch that bit" I replied.

We both then continued to laugh at my misfortune of being a crap bowler,

"See this is what I mean, you have a positive outlook on life, in any situation, it makes me feel more of a positive person." Said Gemma.

Our eyes then met, l looked into those beautiful hazel eyes which even after nearly four months still made my heart melt, she then lent in, and we kissed.

"I'm so glad we got together Mike," Gemma said afterward,

"So am I babe, I have loved you, I mean liked you for so long!" I replied,

"What did you just say? Loved?" Gemma asked.

Panic then set in, my face felt like I was in that hot oven again. I could feel the heat crawling up my neck!

I think Gemma must have seen it too, and that's when she said it!

"Well Mike, I love you too!"

Oh my god, WOW! Did she actually say that? I was surprised by her words as it has been on my mind all week, especially after that damn dream I had. It must have been fate!

"Really? Do you love me? I questioned,

"Yes, I believe I do" she replied confidently,

"I love you to Gemma, I will never forget tonight, not because of the accident on the lane earlier but because of this, because of you." I replied,

"Aw Mike, you're so sweet!" replied Gemma.

We then kissed once more.

We were enjoying our time spent together, so much that we lost track of time, and before we knew it, they were closing the bar and bowling alley.

We headed outside, holding hands, and still laughing to one and other about the 'accident' earlier on that evening, only to be greeted by my mother, with a stern look slapped across her face!

Oh god, I thought to myself, what's her problem now?

As we approached the car, mother greeted Gemma first, not with a stern look, but with one of warmth.

"You had a nice time dear?" Mother asked,

"Yes I have, I think we both have thank you" Gemma replied,

"Mother! Don't say that, it's so cringey to call her dear!" I exclaimed.

Oops, I shouldn't have said that! Her head spun around as fast as an owl, and the expression once again changed to that of annoyance with a tad of anger.

   "Shut up Mike! I'm sure she doesn't mind, and if she does then I won't call her 'dear' again!" She said sternly.

   "No, I don't mind at all" Gemma replied,

   "Well, that's that then! If you're ready to rock and roll, then enter my boudoir of a car!" Said Mother,

   "Oh, God!" I whispered,

It was no boudoir! It was a clapped out Ford Escort that backfired every time mother was in first gear, it never failed to embarrass me! As like right then!

But Gemma didn't seem to mind, she got in first, as me being the gentleman I am, opened the door for her so she could get in first, I got in afterward, Only to be rudely greeted by mother, stating that I never opened the door for her.

   "That is because you are my mother! You are my parent, not my girlfriend!" I stated.

Obviously, this conversation was not helping to sort the issue mother and I had with each other! She was so embarrassing.

As we drove, Gemma and I still held hands, looked at the scenery, which wasn't much to look at, mainly houses and shops, but we enjoyed being in each others company.

We had finally arrived at Gemma house, before leaving the car I reassured her that if she needed to get out of the house because of her arguing parents, that she was always welcome around mine.

"Aw thanks, Mike, I love you."

I statement which had still set off butterflies and making my heart twirl with joy. I replied,

"I love you too."

We had a quick kiss before she got out of the car. What a fantastic evening, well apart from throwing a bowling ball and capturing everyone's unwanted attention, but finally, our relationship was at that next stage, the love stage!

Saturday 15th April 2000

That Saturday, Zoe had decided to throw a last minute party at her house, well, her parents house. Her parents were out for the evening to attend some sort-of business event. She only wanted it to be a small affair so just invited Gemma, Rick, Jay, Graham and me. Gemma had asked Grace if she wanted to come along, but she was staying at her new boyfriend's house for the weekend.

Us lads were running traditionally late, however, that did not stop Gemma and Zoe from getting the party started. Zoe had got hold of some larger, alcopops and a bottle of Gemma's favourite, Malibu!

Zoe was a good source to be able to get alcohol, the lad that had worked at the corner shop had a massive crush on her, so using her flirtatious charm she was able to get served!

Zoe had a right set up going. She had her karaoke machine out and ready to go for when we were all tipsy and daring to sing! Dreadfully, I might add!

All the bottles of alcohol were lined up on her dining room table, ready to be drunk. The girls did not want to wait for us any longer, so they cracked on and opened that bottle of Malibu. They filled the glass 50% Malibu and 50% coke, and just downed it,

   "Christ that was strong" said Gemma as she cringed from its strength.

Gemma had to be a little careful, as much of an amazing young woman she was, she certainly couldn't handle her drink very well! Once, I managed to get her drunk on one can of Stella, the lightweight!

Gemma and Zoe had a couple more high strength drinks and were already starting to feel its great effects, the mood went from a happy, sober kind of atmosphere to a giggly, happy and wanting to dance kind of mood!
So, Zoe put a CD on that was full of all the latest chart songs and turned the volume up. Over the blaring music, Zoe shouted,

   "Whoo, lets dance!"

Gemma got up from the sofa and started to dance with Zoe, both of them trying not to spill their drinks all over Zoe's parents brand new cream carpet!

After 15 minutes or so of dancing and drinking, the inevitable happened.

Gemma and Zoe bumped into each other, which sent Zoe flying into the sofa and then somehow, she rolled over the top of it and fell on the floor behind it! Well, Gemma was in hysterics of laughter, all she could see was Zoe's feet sticking up over the top of the sofa with Zoe laughing away to herself! Who's laugh sounded more like an excited seal! Well, that just made Gemma laugh even harder because of Zoe's incredible howl, she was literally in tears of laughter!

   The laughter was suddenly cut short within an instant when there was a loud banging noise which echoed loudly around the house, loud enough it was clearly heard over the music.

"What was that?" asked Gemma,

"It sounded like it came from the kitchen" replied Zoe.

She turned off the music and both Gemma and Zoe cautiously and slowly walked toward the kitchen,

"Hello, is anyone there? Mike is that you?" Gemma asked.

There was no reply. Surely it was the boys, but why would they slam on something so loudly? Gemma thought.

As they slowly approached the kitchen, Gemma could feel her heart beginning to thump inside her chest. Her hands began to shake with fear. They reached the kitchen, Gemma peered around the door and looked around, there was nobody there, they walked into the kitchen, only to find the back door wide open with the wind howling outside,

"It must have been the wind" said a shaken up Zoe.

Relief engulfed both of the girls, and they started to laugh with the sudden relaxation.

But then! The lights went out! It went pitch black! Both Gemma and Zoe screamed out loudly.

"What the fuck?" shouted Zoe,

"Graham if that's you stop it! You're not funny!" shouted Gemma.

But there was no reply. Zoe scrambled through her draws desperately trying to feel around for a torch, while going through the second draw she found one. She turned it on. Finally, they could see.

"What do we do now?" asked Gemma,

"Come on let's go outside and check the electric box to see if the fuse has gone" replied Zoe.

Zoe cautiously opened the kitchen door which caused a loud, uncomfortable creaking sound as it opened! She stepped outside and looked around, she couldn't see anyone. Gemma followed her out and looked around. Gemma was trembling with fear, struggling to breathe because of the anxiety and adrenaline that was pumping through her body!

It was just a few yards from the kitchen door to the electric box, so not far to walk but it seemed like they were out there for ages.

As Zoe got closer to the electric box she could see that it was open, swinging back and forth with the wind, Zoe looked inside and aimed the torch at the wires. They had been cut!

"Oh my god!" exclaimed Zoe,

"What?" replied Gemma with fear in her voice.

She also looked inside and saw the cut wires, Zoe and Gemma were speechless, they looked at each other with fear in their eyes.

"The guys wouldn't have done this, this is someone else!" Said Zoe who's voice was trembling.

Gemma was speechless. She was in shock. They were both terrified! Gemma looked around once more, There was something in the bushes!

Was it the wind moving through the leaves? She thought.

No, no it was not! There was someone stood watching them!

Gemma screamed out loudly, causing a domino effect with Zoe screaming too, the figure then began to move toward them at a fast pace, Gemma grabbed hold of Zoe's t-shirt and dragged her back inside the house!

Gemma, terrified, locked the door as fast as she could while panicking that she wouldn't be able to secure it quickly enough, but she did, they then ran into the lounge and hid behind the sofa.

It was quiet, too quiet, the only thing they could hear was one and others heavy breathing as they were trying to catch their breath. Somehow Gemma had built up the courage to get up slowly and peer over the sofa to have a look out of the window which was the other side of the lounge.

As she slowly and cautiously peered over, she was stricken with fright! As her eyes fixated on the window, a hooded man was staring right back at her! Frozen with fear Gemma just looked at the man and began to breathe heavily again until her body and mind allowed her to scream out loudly. With her body still frozen the intruder picked up something from the floor and threw it at the window causing it to shatter!

And this is where my part in this evening began.

Jay, Rick, Graham and I were walking along the path just around the corner from Zoe's house, we were all looking forward to the evening that was ahead of us. It wasn't very often that we all had a parent-free opportunity to get drunk, I mean hammered! The only thing that was spoiling it was bloody Graham going on and on about how he was going to invite loads of different girls around, get them drunk and have sex with them all!

"Jasmine! You are so full of shit!" I said to him.

We then got into a friendly argument about how much bull he came out with, and how many times he had proven to be a liar. Jay then commented about how bad the wind was. It was so strong. It was beginning to hold us back from walking.

As we approached Zoe's house, we heard a loud smashing sound which was carried by the wind,

"What the fuck was that?" Asked Jay.

We stood still for a moment but then heard two girls scream out loud!

"That's Gemma screaming!" I shouted.

Without a chance to think about the danger that lay ahead we ran toward Zoe's house, hurdled over the hedge, into her garden and saw that the front window had smashed completely!
We looked around, no one was to be seen.

"What the fuck's happened?" I asked.

My adrenaline was pumping through my veins. I was so worried! I climbed through the window. Incidentally, I cut my hand on a shard of glass! I looked down at my hand and saw the blood seeping out of the cut on my skin! It was so painful, but it didn't bother me! I was too worried about Gemma and Zoe.

I slowly and carefully walked through the lounge closely followed by the guys, we couldn't hear anything, couldn't see anything, so I shouted out,

"Gemma, Zoe where are you? It's Mike!"

I heard a distant voice reply, which sounded like it came from upstairs, it was a female voice. Without fear I ran across the corridor, closely followed by the guys, ran as fast as I could upstairs and stopped on the landing.

"Gemma where are you?" I asked,

"Mike, were in the bathroom, help!" shouted Gemma.

I then ran and smashed through the bathroom door which caused the girls to scream.
Gemma and Zoe were huddled together crying on the floor illuminated by the torch Zoe had in her hand. They were both trembling and crying loudly. I got on the floor with them both and just held them both tightly. I could feel the sweat, heat, and shakiness of their terrified bodies.

"What happened?" I asked,

"I don't know, there was a man" replied Gemma who's voice was still trembling with fear,

"What did he do?" I asked concerning,

"He cut the electrics and then smashed the window with something!" Zoe said through her tears.

Jay and Graham then left the bathroom with Zoe's torch to search for the object that smashed through the window.

"Don't worry, whoever it was has gone, your safe, you have us!" I said,

"I'm so frightened Mike!" Gemma replied while still crying and trembling,

"It's okay sweetheart. I'm here now, and I'll never let anything happen to you" I replied.

From downstairs we heard Jay shout up to us,

"Guy's, you need to see this!"

What was it? I thought, Jay said that with concern written all over his voice, It didn't sound good! Gemma, Zoe, Rick and myself cautiously made our way downstairs, taking it very slowly and carefully as it was pitch black.

Gemma, bless her was holding my hand so tightly it had become numb from the lack of blood supply. We had made it downstairs.

I followed the distant torchlight like a beacon until I got to Jay and Graham who were looking at us with worry written on their faces, Jay was holding something, a piece of paper!

   "What is that?" I asked,

   "Read it mate" Jay replied,

I took the crumpled up piece of paper out of his hand and read it. My face dropped, my heart sank into my stomach, for the first time that night I was frightened, it stated:

'Miller, Gemma, I warned you both to stay away from each other, you ignored me, now it's time to pay the consequence, tonight is just the beginning!'

I looked at Gemma as she had read it too, she looked back at me, both of us gazing at one and other with fear, we didn't know what to think or what to say.

Jay got on the phone to the police to report the incident and to be fair they arrived fast, but what was undoubtedly obvious was that we were all left speechless and frightened, even Graham! The statement that was worrying me the most was the words 'tonight was just the beginning'!

Friday 21st April 2000

Almost a week had passed since the horrific incident at Zoe's house. We were all still shaken up, too frightened to leave our homes. At school, there was a constant police presence, even still, we did not feel safe.

The police had taken fingerprints from the brick that had smashed through the window. It came up with no leads, nothing found from what had cut the electric wires and their prime suspect Franko had vanished off the grid, they couldn't locate him for questioning.

We were all stuck inside our houses after school with nothing to do apart from pondering on what had happened, winding ourselves up with paranoia.

I couldn't take it any longer, staying inside was torturous, so I arranged for Graham and Rick to meet me at Jay's parent's pub so we could have a chat and a catch-up. Each of our parents took us there so we wouldn't have to be out on the streets, I did invite Gemma, but her parents would not let her leave the house which was totally understandable.

Zoe and her parents were staying at her grandmother's house in Essex while the window was waiting to be fixed and to get Zoe away from the area as she seemed to be traumatized with what happened.

At Gemma's house, her parents were arguing ferociously. She was sat on her bed rocking backward and forward listening to all of the shouting coming from downstairs! She was also texting Grace.

Gemma couldn't take it, so she had planned to get out the house discreetly and stay at Grace's sister's home.
With what had happened the previous weekend Gemma had been tipped over the edge, she just wanted to run away from it all. To go away, run away and be on her own. Grace had text back, telling her that she would be at the top of her road in fifteen minutes so that she could pick her up and take her away.

Quickly, Gemma started packing some of her clothes including a photograph of her and myself into a suitcase, but then she was interrupted by her mum who walked into her room.

"What are you doing?" asked her mum,

"Mum, I can't stand all this arguing, I could have been attacked last weekend, and all you and Dad are doing is arguing!" Gemma replied.

Gemma started sobbing.

Gemma's mum sighed, then sat down beside her on the bed, put her arm around Gemma in an attempt to comfort her. Gemma just pushed her mum's hand away.

"You two are so selfish! This has been going on far too long" Gemma shouted through her tears.

Gemma's mum then started crying, both of them looked at each other. They both looked alike, almost like sisters.

"Listen, Gem, your dad and I" she paused,

"Your dad and I are breaking up," she said,

Gemma looked shocked. She guessed this was going to happen but didn't expect it to be that night. She was in disbelief.

"Where are you going to go?" Gemma asked,

"Well, I have arranged for us to stay with my sister, your aunt's house" she replied,

"Oh my god mum, that's over 300 miles away, what about Mike and I? My exams?" Gemma asked frantically.

Gemma's mum explained that she could still carry on dating me, but unfortunately the move would be permanent and that they were going that night! Gemma just shot up like a bolt of lightning with fury in her eyes!

"Tonight, tonight?" Gemma shouted,

"I'm so sorry" Gemma's mum sobbed.

But Gemma had no sympathy, she was shocked and angry, especially as she would not have a proper chance to say goodbye to me.

Gemma had heard enough, angrily she ran out of her bedroom and down the stairs.

"Where are you going?" said Gemma's mum.

But without saying another word, Gemma ran out of the front door and down the street leaving the door ajar.

Gemma's mum, in an attempt to follow her, was stopped by Gemma's dad who explained that they should give her a little space to process the information, that running after her would make things worse.

At the top of the road, Gemma was waiting for Grace to come and pick her up. She was crying her heart out in total shock and disbelief. It was like her heart had been ripped out and stomped on, she didn't know what to think, what to say or what to do! A car then pulled up alongside Gemma, and Grace got out, she ran over to Gemma, hugged her and asked her what had happened.

Gemma let everything out while tears were rolling down her face, she told Grace what her mother had just told her, how frightened she still was after the previous weekend, how Gemma was scared for my safety and that she couldn't cope any longer.

   "Well that's just unfortunate isn't it!" Grace said with a sarcastic tone!

Grace let go of Gemma! Gemma stopped crying.

She looked up at Grace who just stared at her with a sinister smile wiped across her face!

   "What is that supposed to mean?" asked a confused Gemma.

Gemma heard a car door slam shut!

She looked toward the car and saw Franko stood there, smiling!

"Grace what is this about?" Gemma asked.

"Are you really that fucking stupid, how the fuck do you think Franko would know when you were leaving the disco, when you were going to walk down that alleyway and when you were at that party last weekend?" Grace sniggered.

"Grace, I thought we were friends, why are you doing this?" questioned Gemma.

She was shocked, upset and terror replaced tears.
Gemma began to tremble with fear, her heart pounding hard inside her chest, a fight or flight response engulfed her.

"Friends? I fucking hate you" shouted a sadistic Grace.

Franko just stood there with a grin across his thuggish face, enjoying every minute of Gemma's humiliation. Gemma turned to Franko and asked,

"How could you do this? I thought it was all over and done with?"

"Gemma, my darling, it will never be over!" came Franko's sarcastic reply.

Gemma then felt a sudden pain at the back of her head, and everything instantly went dark, she had been knocked out by Grace who hit her over the head with an unknown heavy object.

At the pub, in Jay's living room he, Rick, Graham and myself were all sat on the sofa in unnerving silence, staring into thin air. We had a film on, but we were not paying any attention to it. It had been like that all evening.
We had hardly said a word to each other. Graham was exceptionally quiet. It was the first time in the five years that I had known him to be like that. We were blank, emotionless and traumatized. If this had been Franko's plan all along, he had indeed, succeeded in defeating us.

That silence, suddenly broke when my mobile phone rang out loudly! It made us all jump as we certainly were not expecting it. I took the phone out of my pocket, looked at it and saw that whoever was calling had their number withheld, I answered it,

    "Hello?"

    "Hello Miller!" said a voice in a deep masculine tone which made me feel very nervy,

    "Who is this?" I asked,

    "You're worst fucking nightmare" The voice replied.

I now knew who this was. I knew I recognized that voice! Franko, oh my god it's Franko! I thought. I became nervous, frightened and that familiar sickly feeling overtook me, I whispered to the others,

    "It's Franko, it's Franko."

The guys lent forward with an expression of worry written all over their faces as I spoke. I put the phone on loudspeaker so that the others could hear.

"What do you want Franko?" I asked,

"I want you, Miller, I want you to face me!" Franko snarled.

I was speechless. I did not know what to say. The way he had said it made me terrified and how the hell did he get my number? I asked myself silently.

"Miller, I know you are there, I can hear you fucking breathing, maybe this will make you speak."

I could hear Franko walking over what sounded like broken glass and stone.

"Take that off her mouth now!" Franko shouted to someone that was away from the phone,

"Mike stay away, don't come here, it's a trap!" shouted a female voice!

Oh my god that was Gemma's voice! Panic overwhelmed me.

"Gemma? Gemma? Franko, what have you done?" I shouted.

I looked over at the guys, their jaws had dropped, they couldn't believe what they were hearing, they were listening in despair. Gemma began to scream. I could hear Franko sadistically sniggering. Gemma then stopped screaming. I couldn't hear anything other than Franko breathing.

He came back onto the phone.

"Franko, what the fuck have you done to her? Where is she?" I shouted,

"Miller, Miller, Miller, rewind your puny little neck in, she's safe, for the moment!" He sniggered,

"Let her go please, please let her go. I will do anything you want, just don't hurt her!" I pleaded,

"As I said before, face me, bring your worthless carcass to me, and we will finish this man to man!" He replied,

Jay began shaking his head whispering,

"No, no."

But I had to do it, I couldn't let him hurt Gemma. If I died, then I died I thought to myself.
I knew full well that I would not stand a chance against him in a fist fight, that if he had gone to these lengths to get me to come to him, then I knew that there was one thing, and one thing only on his mind.

"Where do you want me to go?" I replied nervously, dreading his reply,

"The Asylum, that same asylum you dickheads went to. Go to the top floor, fourth room on the right and I'll be there, oh and Miller, if you call the old bill then I will slit your precious girlfriend's throat wide open and watch her blood spill over the floor, you have one hour!"

He then hung up. The phone fell silent. I fell silent.

I stumbled back and fell onto the floor, what do I do? How do I get her out? Were some of the thoughts rambling around in my head.

I looked over to Jay, Rick, and Graham for some kind-of support but they couldn't offer any, I felt alone, defeated.

I sat on the floor shaking with nerves, desperately fighting back a panic attack but I had to do something, I couldn't let him kill her! How am I going to get her out? How am I supposed to walk six miles in an hour? Right think Mike, think! I thought. I had an idea, I could call my cousin, he can handle himself well, and he hates Franko, I thought. While the others were sitting silently in shock, I got up and headed for the door.

   "Where are you going?" asked Jay,

   "I can't just sit here. I am going to get her" I replied with a distinctive tremble in my voice,

   "Dude you can't go alone, you'll stand no chance," Jay said concerning,

   "I'm going to call John and get him to come with me" I replied,

   "Well, if you're going then I'm going!" Jay said confidently.

Jay then stood up, waiting to go,

   "Don't forget me?" Rick said,

   "And me!" Graham said.

They stood up, we walked out of the lounge, but even though I had the backup, I felt unconfident.

I immediately called John and told him what had happened and what Franko's demands were, well John was fuming! I had never heard him that angry in a long time. I asked him if he would help us in our rescue attempt.
Without any hesitation he was in, gunning for his piece of Franko! What was even better for us was that he happened to be driving through the village that we were in, but there was just one problem, how would we get downstairs and walk out of the pub without our parents seeing?

Jay had the perfect solution, quite easily, we could climb out of his bedroom window, hop onto the kitchen's flat roof which was just five feet down then jump down using the kitchen window sill. No one would see us as it was twilight outside and the sky had heavy cloud cover, so it was just about dark.

We did just that. By the time we had got into the car park John was waiting for us, we jumped into his car, and John sped away.

   Twenty minutes later we arrived at the asylum! John had dimmed his lights upon approaching the building in an attempt to mask our approach, but we all knew Franko would know that we were there.
We sat in the darkness of the car for a few moments, carefully scanning the area for any movements or figures from Franko's gang, we couldn't see any.
John turned the car engine off and cautiously, we got out of the car armed with weapons that we had picked up from John's caravan on the way there. We had baseball bats, lead pipes, and empty glass bottles in our armoury.

We were ready, not for a battle, but a war!

John locked his car and had one last look around to make sure that nobody was about and there wasn't. John huddled us together and gave his instructions. We were to follow him inside the building while making sure that we were on the lookout for anyone of Franko's mates, and that he would tell us what to do next once we neared the building.

As we cautiously made our way silently toward the entrance, I became nervous. I felt sick. I was battling with my emotions, silently asking myself, what about this? What about that? But I needed to remain focused, I had to use my anger and my adrenaline to push me through, I needed to find my raw animal instinct.

We reached the entrance, the same door we had used that night when we were there ghost hunting.
John stopped and stood still as he walked inside, my heart began to race, had he seen something or someone?
John turned around and asked if either Graham to Rick would stay behind in the tiny side room to the left. One reason to keep a lookout and the second to call the police once we had reached the top floor.

Rick wanted to do the task, and to be honest, he would be the most reliable. John instructed Rick to text if anyone was to follow us and that Jay would text him for the signal to call the police once we had reached our destination. The plan was simple.

Rick nodded in acknowledgement and let out a puff of air to calm his nerves, and on we went, leaving Rick behind to do his part.

We walked carefully down the long corridor, past where we had gone down into the tunnels previously and headed toward the staircase which leads straight to the top floor. With every room and adjoining corridor, we walked past I made sure that I had a good look in and down every one of them, making sure that nobody was hiding inside.

I had a baseball bat tightly within my grasp in one hand and a glass bottle in the other, ready to swing at full power when the time was right and that time could have come at any moment.

We reached the staircase. John stopped once more. I looked up at the eerie old staircase, knowing full well that danger lies at the top of them. John quietly instructed me to walk up first, get six steps ahead and then the others and John would follow behind. I was now terrified. I was going to bottle it, I felt like running in the opposite direction, I began to breathe heavy in an attempt to fight back a panic attack,

"Mike, listen to me carefully, don't be scared, we are all going to be right behind you, I will personally make sure you won't get harmed!" Whispered John.

That statement reassured me just enough, I mean, just enough to be able to do it. I nodded my head, looked back up the stairs and took a deep breath.

I began to climb, slowly and carefully, trying not to stand on anything that would make a noise. The others were closely following me, I kept a constant eye out for anyone that would attempt to jump us. I could see the top, only four steps left, I slowed down, taking those last few steps at a snail's pace.

I had reached the top, this was it, there was no going back! Just four rooms now stood between me, Gemma and possible death.

John whispered to me,

   "Mike, you going to have to go first, we will be just ten steps behind you."

I was numb, adrenaline and fear had engulfed me, I think if I were in any other situation I would have passed out by this point but I had to keep going, staying strong and focused. I began to walk down the corridor toward the first room on the right.

   I reached door number one - I cautiously peeked my head around it to make sure nobody was there, it was empty, I looked ahead and began to move forward slowly and carefully.

Door number two - Again, I cautiously looked inside, empty again, I couldn't help but notice that it had gone darker, that the atmosphere had somehow changed, it felt still, quiet, electrically charged, and terrifying. I grasped the bat even harder as I carried on walking down the corridor.

Door number three – I looked inside with my baseball bat in the swinging position, ready to hit anybody that was there.

I heard light footsteps! My heart began to race. My hands started to shake!

I took a deep breath in and swung my head around, only to see Jay, John, and Graham's silhouettes come up the stairs to follow me.

I had forgotten that they were there, I felt just slightly more relieved upon realizing that they were behind me, guarding me.

I began to slowly, very slowly make my way toward door number four, my destination.
I remember hoping Jay had remembered to text Rick to give him the signal to call the police.

I stopped just a foot or two before I reached the room. I needed to sort myself out. I was falling apart once more. I closed my eyes and took a few silent breaths in. I desperately tried to compose myself and keep my thoughts clear, I just repeated over and over in my mind: Focus, fight, Gemma, focus, fight, Gemma.

Door number four – My destination, I took a deep breath in, and I just slowly went in without stopping as I knew that if I had hesitated, I would not have been able to do it.
I was in the room. It seemed more extensive than I expected. There was a little bit of light from the distant street lamps, but not much, so I had a little bit of light, just enough to see, but I couldn't see anything, I couldn't see anyone, what was going on?

As I cautiously walked on I began to realize that the room was in a shape of an 'L' there was a wall in front of me, so I crept up to the edge of it. I looked back toward the door and saw the guys walk through, they too, slowly and cautiously following me.

I slowly, very slowly peered around the corner.

There she was, I could see her!
Tied to a chair in the center of the room, she looked as if she was unconscious.

Sadness overwhelmed me. Tears began to well up in my eyes, I had become emotional, I lost composure.

Without thinking, I dropped my metal bat onto the floor which made a loud crashing sound as it hit the deck and I ran to her. With tears in my eyes, I tried to wake her.

"Gemma wake up, Gemma wake up!" I whispered.

I began to shake her to in a desperate attempt to wake her. As I was trying to untie her, I heard footsteps coming from behind me. I assumed it was the guys,

"MIKE! WATCH OUT!" Jay shouted!

I spun around, I saw a figure stood over me swinging a baseball bat at me, I leaped to my left!
The bat narrowly missed me as it blasted the ground with force.

The man, dressed in all black and wearing a balaclava lifted the bat above his head and swung again.

As the bat was about to crush my skull, Jay rugby tackled the unknown man and took him to the ground. Jay then hit him, hard over the head with sheer rage with his lead pipe. Jay had knocked him out.

Was it Franko? I certainly was not going to hang around to see it was.

John was already cutting the rope that Gemma had tied to her. When another hooded man came hurtling toward us! This time Graham took him out!

He hit him in the chest with a plank of wood, then began to kick the hooded gang member in the face and ribs until he laid still and motionless on the floor. Well, that was some beating Graham just gave, I didn't realize he had it in him! But how many others were there? I thought.

As John untied Gemma she awoke,

   "Mike, Mike" she muttered.

I ran over to her and knelt down in front of her.

   "Gemma it's me, I'm here, you're safe now" I said,

   "Thank god Mike, please get me out of here" she murmured.

Still, in a daze, John picked her up and carried her out of the room, ran along the corridor and down the stairs as fast as we could go.

We were on our final straight. We could see the exit. We were sprinting as fast as we could, safety was just around the corner.

BANG! - A gunshot!

I felt the air from the bullet which narrowly missed my face as it came skimming by me. I looked around, stood in the shadows was Franko.
We stopped running, we turned and faced the monster who was confidently pointing his handgun directly at us. He started to take steps toward us, so we slowly took steps backward, just a matter of yards from the exit.

"Where the fuck do you think you are going?" Franko sniggered,

We didn't say anything back to him, we just nervously stepped backward with each step he took toward us.

"What's up, cat got your fucking tongue Miller! Well come on then hard man, face me!"

"No" I angrily replied,

"No? Fucking no! You fucking pussy! You worthless piece of shit! No wonder she wants to fucking leave you!" Franko shouted,

"What do you mean?" I replied,

"She was going to leave you tonight, run away, never to return!" Franko shouted.

He seemed drunk, even high on drugs or maybe he had just lost it. I could see his piercing eyes through the aim of his gun. They were wide. They looked wholly dilated, possessed, he had turned psychotic.

"That's not true Franko, and you know it isn't, your just twisting things!" Shouted Gemma,

"Oh no I'm not, go on Gemma tell you're pathetic boyfriend the truth!" He sniggered,

I turned to Gemma.

"Gemma, what does he mean?" I asked,

"Mike, my mum, and dad, MIKE WATCH OUT!" she shouted.

I turned my head sharply! Franko was sprinting toward me with a large knife in his hand! I froze! I closed my eyes then the impact came! I was shoved ferociously into the wall with force, but there was no pain, no nothing, I could hear gargling, a gargling type of noise.

I opened my eyes! I was horrified! It was Rick!

He must have jumped in front of him at the last second. I looked at him. He looked in pain, terrible pain! His eyes fixated and widened with fear. He opened his mouth slightly, and blood came trickling out, slowly at first but then suddenly began to gush out!

He leaned into me and fell to the floor with his eyes wide open, not moving, not breathing, just choking on his blood.

I fell to the floor with him then I heard a scream, a raging scream!

I looked up into the darkness and Franko came charging at me through it with the knife in hand!

He was a couple of feet away from me when Jay struck him with my baseball bat, right around the head and knocked him completely out.

I was in shock, disbelief I was stunned! Was this real?

I could hear screaming and shouting, but everything seemed muffled.

I stood up then looked down at the floor. John and Graham were desperately trying to revive Rick, giving chest compressions and mouth to mouth.
I looked to my right, Jay was holding Gemma who was crying and not knowing what to do, she looked to me, then ran to me, I held her tightly.

"Please, don't die, please don't die!" She cried out.

John ordered Graham to step away as he took over, giving Rick chest compressions. Things were getting desperate. He was not responding.

I could hear sirens, lots and lots of sirens. I looked outside and could see the blue flashing lights draw nearer.
Jay and Graham ran out to grab the attention of the police and paramedics by waving their arms in the air.
I turned around and looked at Gemma. She looked at me, her eyes reddened by the tears, so I held her so very tightly once more, in an attempt to comfort her. I looked back down at an exhausted John trying to save Rick who was lying lifeless on the floor surrounded by a pool of blood.

By the time the paramedics had got to him, it was too late. He had gone, Rick was dead!

After that, everything was just a blur. I can't remember leaving the building or what happened to Jay, Graham, and John. All I knew was that the police took us all away separately to take statements.

After half an hour of receiving attention from the paramedics in the back of an ambulance and giving a statement to the police, it still had not sunk in about what had happened, Rick was dead, but it didn't feel like he was. It felt surreal, confusing, like a bizarre, frightening dream that I just wanted to wake up from, to wake up and everything to be as it was.

I got a clean bill of health from the paramedic who was attending to me, so I went off to find Gemma. She was in the ambulance in front of me receiving stitches from the cut on the back of her head.

I waited outside of the ambulance for her as was her mum. We did not say anything to each other as I just assumed both of us was in shock about what had happened.
After a couple of minutes of uncomfortable silence, the door opened, Gemma had finally been let out.

"Hey" I said softly.

She couldn't even look at me, she did not answer me.
She just began to sob. She asked her mum to leave us alone for a few minutes, but she was reluctant, she didn't want to leave Gemma's side. Gemma assured her mum that police were everywhere and that everything was safe.

"I'll give you two a couple of minutes." Her mum said nervously.

She walked away leaving Gemma and myself together.

"Are you okay?" I asked – again, she didn't answer me.

"Hey, come here," I said as I attempted to hug her.

She just pushed me away and started to cry! She had never done this before. I was so worried about her. I assumed that it was because of what had happened, that she was in shock.

"I can give you space babe if you need it?" I asked,

"It's not that," she said through streams and streams of tears,

"What is it, babe? You can tell me. I love you" I replied concerning.

Gemma started to cry even harder. I had never seen anybody so upset and distraught in all of my life, not even to this day. It was so heartbreaking to watch, but she wouldn't let me near her, I just desperately wanted to comfort her. She struggled, but managed to compose herself.

"I can't do this anymore Mike" She stuttered,

"It's okay. It's all over with now. He'll be locked away. Things will get better" I replied,

"I don't mean that I'm sorry, so sorry!"

She began to cry again, her body shook with anxiety.

"What do you mean then?" I asked worryingly,

"Mike, my parents, have broken up, we're moving away, and with everything that's happened I just need to be on my own, make a fresh start, forget about everything!" She shouted through her tears.

I felt tears well up in my eyes. I was speechless!

I too began to tremble, I felt sick to the stomach so much I thought I was going to be sick.

It began to rain, slow at first but quickened its pace, getting faster and harder until it had turned extremely heavy. Almost instantly we were both soaked. Neither of us moved. We just stood still looking into one and others eyes.

"What does this mean for us?" I asked while looking into those tear-filled hazel eyes with rainwater streaming down her face.

"I'm sorry, but this is it, Mike, its over," she said softly.

Her face then screwed up, she was trying so hard to resist the tears as she walked away leaving me frozen with shock.

I just stared into the pounding rain, a blank space from where she had just been stood, for what seemed like minutes.
I looked to my left, Gemma and her mother was getting into a police car.

I suddenly realized what was going on. It had sunk it! She was breaking up with me! I couldn't let her go, after all we had been through I just couldn't let her go.

I ran toward the police car as it started driving away, I ran
faster and faster trying to keep up!
I saw Gemma turn around and look out of the back window.
All I could see was an upset, traumatized, beautiful face
looking at me with tears just rolling down it.

I couldn't keep up, I sprinted and sprinted until I physically
could not run any longer which caused me to be sick.

She was gone! It was over!

My whole world instantly came crashing down around me! I
could literally feel the weight of the sky and what is beyond
weighing down on my back, pushing me to the floor.
I collapsed into the mud, and I just cried, roaring with despair!
Everything I had fought for was to no avail. My friend was
dead, the love of my life, ripped away from me, my life, my
entire life, destroyed!

So there I was, Mike Miller, a 16-year-old SINGLE guy, laying
in a puddle of rainwater and mud! My life torn apart, hopes and
dreams ripped away! Not even being able to contemplate
where I went from there.

A Misguided Guide
of a
30-something
DAD

I AM
SMILER

UP COMING NOVELS

Love's *TWISTED* Diary 2

PLUS MORE TO BE ANNOUNCED.

Please keep an eye on my Facebook page for announcements and updates.

Facebook.com/krisdeanwriter

Printed in Great Britain
by Amazon